THE PROTECTOR'S PROMISE

BORDER SERIES BOOK SEVEN

CECELIA MECCA

ALTIORA
PRESS

To Border Series readers. Thank you.

THE LEGEND

While beautiful and ethereal in her wildness, Scotland held within her so much power, she could very well tear herself apart. To ensure Scotland's safety, an ancient order of druids decided to safeguard her very heart.

They made a stone of the purest emerald green, protected by a necklace wrought of gold and iron, and locked her soul within it, imbuing the stone with magical properties no mortal could ever destroy. For every generation to come, the soul of the stone would select a protector, a woman with a pure heart and the ferocity of a warrior. Upon her death, the immortal stone would then seek the security of its next protector. But the battle of light and dark is as old as time, and nature has a way of balancing itself—whether for good or evil.

When the reach of the stone stretches toward its next guardian, so too does the call go out to the opposing force—a man whose heart is set on reclaiming Scotland for his own purposes. Both guardian and nemesis receive their mark and are drawn toward the stone that lies in wait within the glittering shallows of the fairy pools guarded by the Priestess of the Stone.

Scotland's darkest days will emerge if the stone should fall into the wrong hands. The fate of the chosen is a never-ending battle for the stone, Scotland's lifeblood, between the protector and her adversary. For when one dies, a new struggle will begin again until the end of time.

Isle of Skye, Scotland, 1273
"Give me a reason not to kill you."

With the tip of his broadsword to his attacker's throat, the Lord of Camburg stood immobile, waiting for the Scotsman's answer. The guard stared back at William.

No response.

He tried again. "What are you guarding?"

Nothing.

He'd not traveled all this way, from the borderlands of North West England, to be stopped so close to his goal.

Suddenly, the big, bearded man who'd tried to lop off William's head from behind shifted before his eyes. A scared young boy, too young to grow a beard, lay in his place. The vision disappeared, and William found himself staring once again at the man who had followed him from the moment he'd begun his ascent up the mountain. The winding path had hidden his pursuer from sight, but the silence had done nothing to mask the big man's telltale footfalls.

The visions came more often now. He had gone years without them, but since arriving in Scotland, they occurred nearly every day. Most often, they were altered versions of that which was in front of him and other times of what was to come. Perhaps whatever was at the top of this mountain might provide some much-needed answers. He hoped so since they were becoming harder and harder to disguise.

Though he would likely regret it, William pulled back his sword. The fleeting visions that had plagued him his entire life had come more readily each day of this voyage. They showed him glimpses of the past or the future, and after seeing the lad the guard had been, he could not harm him. Sheathing his weapon, he moved away from the guard, who scrambled to his feet.

"I am guarding no one," the man insisted.

He lied.

"We shall see." William pointed to the path ahead of them. "Lead the way."

They had nearly arrived. He knew neither what nor whom he sought, something he would never willingly admit to his friends or foes. They'd think he'd descended into madness if he told them, and William may be inclined to agree. But the call that had taken him away from Camburg Castle across the borderlands and to this mountain had been too strong to ignore. Now, after days of aimless wandering with only the strange pull to guide him, William was close.

This man's presence told him as much.

"If you attempt to harm her, I will kill you," the Scotsman said as he picked his way along the rocky path.

"*Her?*"

The guard spun around, his brows furrowed. "Who are you?"

Finally, perhaps, he could get some answers. "An answer for an answer."

The guard responded with a curt nod.

"Who do you protect?"

"Scotland." He answered so quickly, William would have been inclined to believe him if not for the outrageousness of his response. Then again, he'd come here alone, for no better reason than he'd felt drawn to. There was no denying his situation was outrageous.

"Who do you protect"—he pointed—"up there?"

"Scot—"

"You are telling me Scotland resides at the top of this mountain on the Isle of Skye?" He was losing patience. After days of questions with no answers, he was ready for real information. "Try again."

"The Priestess of the Stone. But you knew that already."

Priestess? Stone? What had he stumbled his way into?

All the same, he was a man of his word—he'd promised to answer the man's question in exchange for information. "I am William Thornhurst, son of Lord Ranville and seneschal of Camburg Castle."

"Why are you here?" The man's hands itched at his sides, reaching for a sword that was no longer there.

"I don't know," he answered honestly. Though he had dozens of questions to ask—Who was this priestess? What was the significance of the stone? Why had he been drawn to this secluded place?—the guard's expression threw him off. The man looked at him as if he'd just seen him for the first time before averting his eyes and looking around frantically, as if searching for an escape.

"An answer for an answer," he reminded the guard. "Why do you look at me that way?"

The man's chin lifted. "You will find out soon enough."

With that, he turned away once again and ran ahead. If he hoped William would follow, running headlong into some trap, he would be disappointed. Instead, he continued to make his way up the mountain, listening and waiting. This was not his land, and the guard's knowledge of the terrain would be a profound advantage for him should he decide to make another attack.

William should not have let him live.

The irrepressible urge to come to this place had begun the

morning he'd awoken with that odd mark on his hip. Appearing while he'd slept and seemingly in the shape of a small dagger, the mark ushered a new reality into his life, one filled with the visions of his youth. Nothing had made sense since. Though his men were not surprised he'd wanted to travel alone up north, they'd insisted on joining him. And so William had snuck off under the cloak of darkness, driven by fleeting visions of his destination—the renowned pools of Skye. The visions had served him well in the past, and so he trusted them now once again.

William stopped, the sound of a waterfall ahead drowning out everything else. He could be more easily ambushed now, so he forced himself to slow his steps. Turning another corner, his eyes bulged at the sight before him.

Was it from this world?

Though the oak trees that dotted the landscape had become smaller as he ascended the mountain, one in front of him stood tall and proud next to a waterfall, defying logic. The coloring of the pools at the foot of the small falls baffled him—he'd never seen such shades of green and blue in nature—and the moss-covered rocks that cradled the pools appeared almost unnatural in their smoothness.

A woman stood at the center of them.

Her hooded, dark green cape revealed nothing more than the lower portion of her face and narrowed eyes. The guard that had fled earlier stood by her side, eyeing him warily.

William approached them with equal wariness, watching the lady's back straighten as the guard spoke to her. The waterfall drowned out their words, but he didn't need to hear them talk to notice the change in her expression. It hard turned almost . . . murderous.

"Stop there," she called, the lilt of her voice what he imagined a siren's call would sound like. Oddly, he heeded her bidding.

"Go," she said over the sound of the water descending into the pools below. "Go back to England. Forget this place."

Did she really believe he'd traveled this far only to turn back? He needed answers!

"Why did you call me here?"

The words made no sense, even to his own ears. As he said them, memories flashed before him as clearly as if they'd just happened to him. His father introducing him to Sir Richard. The look on Richard's face when he told William his father had died, leaving him an orphan. The first time he met Lady Sara, the girl who'd been his childhood companion, the girl who was too fine of a lady for a lowly baron's son to wed. Richard granting him Camburg. His visits to court. His dream of attaining his own title, one not handed to him by an indulgent overlord . . .

The priestess watched as the memories pounded through him, each leaving behind enough emotion to bring him to his knees.

"Tell me what it means," he demanded, knowing somehow that she would not.

"Go," she shouted, the word etching itself into his very soul.

Instead, he took a step toward her . . . and then saw it.

Disguised as a regular rock, the gray stone in the center of the shallow pool at her feet gleamed a brighter green than anything found in the natural world. She had not called to him. That stone had summoned him, as mad as that sounded. She did not want him to know it was there, and while it had already turned back to gray, William had seen it for what it was: a relic. One that would help him on a mission that he should be back at Camburg preparing for even now. The king's regent would not be happy if he learned of William's journey. But somehow, when he saw the stone, he knew it would help him capture Moordon Castle.

He jumped into the pools, stumbling toward the stone before the priestess or her guard could even realize his intent. Grabbing the stone, William ran faster than he'd ever run in his life. As he navigated roots and pebbles, nearly falling down the steep incline, William did not pause to look for his pursuer, though it did surprise him that the man hadn't yet caught up. Instead, he made his way as quickly as possible down the mountain, anxious to get away from it all.

The guard . . . the priestess . . . this island. Away from Scotland and the strange forces that had drawn him there.

"My lady," one of Marion's guards called from behind, "there is nothing here but more trees and rocks. We should turn back."

She'd heard that same refrain for the last hour, and Marion was no more inclined to do so now than she had been earlier despite that she felt the stone's pull less now than she had earlier in the day.

Since embarking on this journey, the men who had been told to follow her orders had done everything but. She'd invoked her father's name, her mother's admonitions, and every other argument she could think to make.

Yet, as men were wont to do, they simply refused to listen. So she had stopped trying to convince them. Forging ahead of each of the men sent to protect her, Marion wound her way around the muddy path leading toward her destiny.

And then it was there before her.

"Priestess of the Stone . . . ," Kenneth muttered as he nearly knocked her over from behind. She supposed it was her fault for stopping so abruptly. But at least Marion could cease trying to convince the men, most especially her father's captain, of the existence of the Priestess of the Stone. For standing in front of them, just under a massive oak tree that should not have stood so tall this far up, was the very woman they'd journeyed here to find.

Some said her hair was the same color as Marion's, a flaming red not often found even in these parts. Others believed the priestess was an old woman, her wisdom a testament to her advanced age. Neither tale had any truth to it, for the priestess had flung back the hood of her cape, revealing black, flowing hair.

At least one aspect of the stories was true—the woman who guarded the heart of Scotland, the stone that would be entrusted to Marion, was beautiful.

Marion felt surprisingly calm as she made her way toward the priestess. Her mother had assured her that she had nothing to fear, but she'd always wondered how she could know such a thing. The legend was, after all, just that. No one had met the priestess before, and her location had always been a well-guarded secret. Until now.

"Come," the priestess said, the soft lilting voice comforting her.

Marion obeyed, walking around the glittering blue and green pools to reach the priestess, who held out her hands. She chanced a glance over her shoulder. Her guards were gaping at them, their mouths hanging open.

Instead, Marion placed her hands on top of the priestess's outstretched ones. They were so soft and smooth, just like the even tone of her voice.

"I've been waiting for you."

"My mother bade me come," she said, her tongue heavy and awkward. "The mark appeared on my hip, and I was drawn here." Just as the legends foretold, it was the shape of a small dagger. It had appeared after a strange rumbling shook the earth. After four and twenty years of hearing the tales, Marion had understood at once.

The previous protector had died. She was being called to take the woman's place.

Back home, at Ormonde Castle, Marion had sometimes been accused of being haughty rather than poised, but standing next to this priestess, she felt like a young child, her words forming slowly and awkwardly.

"A wise woman," the priestess said. "We've much to discuss, and quickly." She glanced down at the pools. "The stone has been taken."

7

Had the priestess not held her hands firmly, she may have fallen at that declaration. "Taken?"

Marion followed the woman's gaze and saw nothing but calm, green-hued water and rocks in the pool at her feet. She glanced then at the guard who stood not far from them.

The priestess tugged on her hands. "Aye. And there's much for you to learn. But as I said, there is no time. You must act quickly to recover the stone."

Marion allowed her hands to drop when the priestess let them go.

"You have been chosen as Scotland's protector. Now that you've been summoned to protect it, the dark forces that oppose us, that oppose *you*, have stirred to life once more. I know not why it happened, only that it has."

Marion didn't understand. She'd never heard there was another side to the ancient tale. Her mother had said nothing of dark forces. Of anyone else trying to take possession of the stone.

"An Englishman by the name of William Thornhurst. He took the stone and disappeared earlier today," she explained. "You can detect malintent, can you not?"

"Aye, or at least, I believe so. I have always been able to sense when someone wishes harm to myself or someone I love. 'Tis why my mother was not surprised to see the mark. She always believed I would be the next Protector of the Stone, knowing each garners a special ability from it."

"I do not understand this man's ability, but he was able to recognize the stone from where it was hidden, disguised as an ordinary rock. Though without my enchantment, it will now appear as it is, a precious emerald hanging from a chain of gold."

Now Marion knew why the priestess continued to glance down into the pools.

"He has likely returned to England. To Camburg Castle. You must find him and recover the stone. He will reveal his purpose before two moons pass, so you must act quickly. Trust the stone or—"

"Scotland will suffer." Her duty was clear, and Marion would not disappoint the priestess. Or her parents. Or Scotland. She would recover the stone from this Englishman before the time was up.

"Be careful," the priestess said. "He is smart and strong. And—" She hesitated.

"And?" Marion prompted her.

"Handsome."

She nearly asked, *Why should that matter?* but held her tongue.

"Do not be deceived by him. The last time the stone fell into the hands of an Englishman, Scotland's king lost Northumbria to King Henry."

"Surely that was not because—"

"The fate of our land rests on the possession of that stone."

The priestess was so confident and serious, Marion did not doubt the truth of her words.

Marion surprised herself by taking her advisor's hands once again and squeezing them.

"I will recover the stone and protect it for the remainder of my days," she said. "I will not disappoint you."

For the first time since they met, the priestess smiled. As did Marion.

She had meant every word.

_____

2

"*L*ady Marion?"

Though the leader of her guard, Kenneth, had been more receptive to her orders since the pool, he clearly found it difficult to accept the idea that she was in charge. Marion liked to think it was because he'd known her since she was a young girl and not because she happened to be a woman. She'd tried hard to remain patient, but her patience was running out.

"We must not stop," she repeated, looking around in horror as the men set up camp. "My mother—"

"Is not here," he muttered.

Marion often wondered why, if she could sense malintent, the gruff captain did not give her the familiar sensation of cold washing over her body. The strange bouts of cold chills had scared her as a child until she'd discovered the pattern to them. Since then, she'd been revered—by her parents, their people, by everyone who mattered—for her unique ability. The captain, however, did not seem to share their respect. Perhaps the reason she didn't feel any malintent was that he believed he was serving her best interests. Even so . . .

Mustering her best imitation of her father, the powerful

Scottish border lord whom none would think to question, Marion approached the overly large captain. "Either we continue riding or we risk losing him. And once he reaches Camburg Castle—"

"We have no way of knowing how far ahead—"

"If we continue through the night, we will catch him by morning," she said forcefully.

Even though he'd been told to follow her orders, and he'd now seen the priestess and the pools with his own eyes, Kenneth frowned. He was going to deny her once again.

"You don't know that."

Marion could argue. She could attempt to convince him. But how could she possibly make the stubborn, overly practical Scotsman understand she could sense the stone? As soon as she left the glen, its pull had tugged her in a new direction—the feeling as undeniable as the fact that this conversation was not getting them any closer to their destination.

Instead, she yawned. A fake yawn that turned very real—they'd set a brutal pace since leaving Skye. And still, the Englishman eluded them.

Well, no longer. "Perhaps you are right," she lied.

And without further discussion, Marion pulled the bedroll from her mount and followed the guard's lead. If Kenneth looked at her strangely, it was because he was unused to her acquiescence. And, may the saints forgive her, she was so driven by desperation, she was about to do the very thing she'd promised her parents never to do.

The guards would be furious when they realized she'd ridden off alone.

As would her parents, but luckily they were back home, safe in their beds, while she battled her fear of the dark. When she finally untied her mount and made her way to the edge of camp, Marion stopped one last time. This close to the border, many dangers lay ahead. But none terrified her as much as human predators,

11

namely reivers. Scottish, English . . . it mattered not. Either might do her harm.

"Truly, lass? You would travel across the border, at night, alone?"

Consarn it. "I'm not sure what you mean?"

The captain was not amused.

"Kenneth, please listen to me. Do you not believe I . . . know things . . . even though I wish it were not so?"

"My lady—"

"I've no wish to navigate this land alone, but you refuse to heed me," she said. She needed to make him understand. The pull toward the stone became stronger with every step, and somehow she just *knew* if they kept going—

"Very well."

Kenneth managed to surprise her.

"You will get yourself killed if you ride off alone," he mumbled. Then he shouted to the others, most of whom were apparently already awake. "We leave, now."

Marion smiled, grateful she would not be forced to extreme measures. And although their path was only lit by moonlight and their pace was slow, their efforts were rewarded.

Just beyond a thicket of trees, barely discernible but growing larger as she approached, stood a lone figure beside a horse. Without a word to Kenneth or the others, Marion spurred her mount forward, for she knew at once this was William Thornhurst, the Englishman who'd stolen the Stone of Scotland. *Her* stone. Or rather, her countrymen's stone and the one that would bring peace and prosperity to them. She felt it pulling her closer.

When she was nearly upon the thief, he pulled out his sword.

Would he kill a woman?

When she halted in front of him and dismounted, Marion thought two things at once.

The cold had not gripped her as she'd expected it would.

And the priestess had been right . . . he was quite handsome.

It was only when the riders behind her came into view that William drew his sword. Four men following a woman.

Though not just any woman.

A redheaded, green-eyed beauty who appeared as if she'd like nothing better than to murder him.

"Give me the stone," she demanded in a seething voice. He couldn't reconcile her voice, so commanding and low for a woman, with the smattering of freckles across her nose. Had the priestess sent this group after him?

Her guards were getting too close. Four. I need an advantage.

Without hesitating, he reached out and grabbed the Scotswoman—her accent left no doubt that she was one—and spun her around. Just as her men approached, he lifted his sword until it hovered just beneath her chin.

"That's close enough," he shouted. Not surprisingly, her men stopped far enough away to give him a few moments to consider his next move.

"Let go of me!" The way she twisted in his arms and brushed her bottom against him made William suddenly wish he wore a hauberk. This was not a convenient time for an arousal, though he could certainly understand his body's response.

"Stop moving," he whispered in her ear. "Or I will kill every one of your men."

She complied. Perhaps she assumed he meant those words, though in truth he did not. Though he did need the stone, even if he did not understand why.

Rather than cower, however, as a woman in her position should do, the woman lifted her chin and continued to issue orders.

"Give me the stone," she demanded.

"A bad idea, old man," William shouted to the apparent leader of the guards, who had begun to dismount. He tightened his grip against the redheaded woman.

"You have two choices," he tried to reason with her. "Forget the stone, and ride off with your men when I release my grip. Otherwise, you're coming with me." It was the only way he'd maintain any kind of advantage.

She apparently did not care for either choice.

Turning to her men, she shouted, "He's not going to—"

He moved his hand swiftly from her shoulder to cover her mouth. When she tried to bite him, his gloves prevented any damage.

Moving toward his horse, William thought of how best to get them mounted and away from her guards. He envisioned each possible maneuver—and its follow-through—and decided in a trice. Once again, he did not hesitate. With his sword arm, he grabbed the horse's reins, and he swung himself up with his other hand, never releasing his grip on the woman. Blocking out the sounds of her guards' advance, he sheathed his sword and pulled her up and in front of him.

"Continue to squirm and you'll fall. Sit still . . . you may survive the day."

Thankfully, it was enough to stop her. For now. But the others were nearly upon them. And though William had crossed the border into England earlier that day, this was not a familiar path to him. Looking for an escape, he relied on speed to put distance between himself and his would-be attackers.

There!

The old Roman road split just ahead. As soon as the others rode over the ridge behind them, her men would see which path they took . . . unless they were already long gone. But which path *should* he take? The main road? Aye. They would likely think he'd take the one less traveled.

His eye judged that he'd taken the turn just in time to lose them.

But he kept going at a gallop, working under the assumption the pursuers were just behind him. He only slowed after riding for what seemed like hours, though he knew from the sun's position it had not been so long.

"They'll kill you when they find us."

"They are welcome to try."

For the first time since he whisked her onto his horse, the Scotswoman turned to look at him. A pert nose. Full lips. Her outfit and demeanor told him she was a lady, and a brave one at that.

"Why did you take the stone?"

"Why do you want it back?"

She turned back around, the unladylike huff prompting his next impertinent question.

"You the daughter of . . . whom exactly? A great border lord? Perhaps the king of Scotland himself?"

"My father," she spat out, "is an earl."

"Ahh," he mocked. "An earl. Of course."

"He is no castellan." Her taunt hit too close to the mark. His relatively lowly position had made it impossible for him to marry another earl's daughter . . .

"You never answered my question," she said. "What does the Lord of Camburg want—"

"How do you know who I am?" Her words surprised him for a moment, but hadn't he guessed she had some connection to the priestess? "The priestess sent you." He didn't expect a response, but as the road narrowed and wound its way through a thicket of trees, she answered anyway.

"She did not *send* me. The stone you carry is rightfully mine. It belongs to Scotland. It belongs—"

"You know what it is?"

"You don't?" She turned around again, and by God, if she kept doing that, he'd be near crippled with desire by the time they made it back to Camburg. He'd obviously been too long without a woman. "Then why did you take it?"

When she blinked, her dark lashes kissed the creamy skin beneath. William had never kidnapped a woman before, but he found it was an exceedingly difficult task. The last time he'd been this distracted by a woman . . . in fact, he had never experienced anything like this.

His only answer was not much of one at all. "It . . . called to me."

Her eyes widened. "That's it? You really don't know?" Then something changed in her expression. Whereas it had been angry before, it softened. And then, unfortunately, she turned back around.

"Will you tell me?" he heard himself asking.

"Aye," she said. "I will. But you must promise to give it back—"

"I cannot tell you why, only that I know that I need it."

Her shoulders slumped. "Then I tell you nothing."

He'd expected as much. "Will you at least tell me your name?"

She folded her arms in front of her, forcing him to tighten his grip lest she fall off the horse.

"You know mine. At least—"

"Lady Marion, daughter of Archibald Rosehaugh, 3rd Earl of Ormonde."

Right. An earl's daughter. And an only child like Sara, no doubt.

"Court," he responded.

She turned again. "Pardon?"

"Court. My given name is indeed William, but I've gone by the name of Court since coming to Camburg."

"Court," she repeated. "As in—"

"Aye, the king's court," he said, preparing for her laughter, which surprisingly never came.

"I'd give you leave to call me Marion," she said. "But since I am your captive—"

"Marion." He said it as much to infuriate her as to test the name on his lips. He was not disappointed.

"*Lady* Marion. Or better—"

"Marion," he repeated. "You are not my captive for long. When we return to Camburg and your men arrive, I will happily give you over to them."

"Lady Marion," she corrected. "And how are you so confident my men will not find us before then?"

Court leaned down to whisper in her ear. "Because, *Marion,* I've no wish to be found. And when I want something, I get it."

3

*H*e obviously thought highly of himself.

Marion was not accomplishing anything by demanding he relinquish the stone. He'd refused to give it to her more than once, not that she'd really expected he would simply hand it over. But it was clearly time for a new plan.

"Court," she said sweetly, imitating her flirtatious cousin and trying not to laugh at the poor effort, "do you perhaps have anything to eat?"

Though they'd stopped once to see to their needs, she and her captor had spent the remainder of the day on horseback. And though she no longer feared for her life, Marion was hungry, tired, and more than a little annoyed.

"When we camp for the night, I'll catch something for us. And Marion?"

"Yes, Court?" She found she rather liked the sound of his common name on her lips.

"It won't work."

She could have feigned ignorance, but it wasn't worth the effort. Frustrated, she silently railed against her "special ability." For something so unique and special, it was really of no use to her at all. Not when she hadn't felt the slightest chill since meeting her nemesis, who was surely the most dangerous person alive at the moment.

Giving up, she tried for a more practical approach. "What are your intentions?"

"With you," he said, shifting behind her, "or the stone?"

She shifted as well, trying to find a comfortable position.

"Stop," he growled out.

Marion turned, trying to understand what she'd done wrong now. "I didn't do—"

His expression forced her mouth closed. She swallowed, knowing that look. Too many suitors had sought her favor over the years for her not to understand desire when she saw it. Refusing to look away, Marion stared into a set of hazel eyes that looked more blue than green or brown. With a square jaw and short, blondish-brown hair, her Englishman was no less handsome than when they'd met earlier that day. And the way he looked at her . . .

Marion spun back around.

"Your intentions with me," she said finally.

"I already told you, I intend—"

"But we are not near Camburg," she pointed out. "It will take—"

"Just one more full day of riding. We are closer than you think."

Marion knew enough of England to know Camburg was just below the border, but she'd lost track of where they were exactly. Now that the stone was within her reach, nothing guided her forward except . . . well, him.

"As for the stone, I have no intentions toward it. I know only that it belongs to me. It pulled me toward it, and I had no choice but to listen."

Marion did not bother arguing with him. She knew exactly what he meant by that, even if he did not. They had ridden past the thicket of trees and now made their way through a wide-open field. She watched as the sun began to dip below the horizon.

"Why are there no other travelers? Where are we?"

"We've ventured off the main road." Court pointed to their right. "Your companions are likely west of us, but they'll eventually circle back as they approach Camburg."

"We're off the main road?"

"Aye, we have been for some time now."

She looked down, and while there were few hoof marks beneath them, it appeared very much as if the road was well traveled.

"Have you ever left Ormonde?"

"Of course." In fact, she had not, with the exception of this journey. She'd begged to visit Edinburgh many times, of course, but her parents had claimed it was much too dangerous given the possibility she was "Scotland's chosen one." Heaven and the saints above forbid anything should happen to her.

Then, when the mark appeared, they finally trusted her to know where to go and what to do . . . and here she was, the prisoner of some English knight intent on— "You're planning an attack?"

If he was the opposing force, according to the priestess, he would be the one to throw Scotland into chaos if he kept the stone. Which meant Scotland would suffer so long as it remained in his hands. And according to the priestess, the suffering would begin within two moons of his possession of the stone.

His silence was all the answer she needed.

"Where?" she demanded. "When?"

Court stopped the horse and dismounted, reaching up for her. She pushed away his hand and followed him down without any assistance despite the size of his destrier. She followed Court and his massive black warhorse toward the sound of rushing water.

"Are we stopping for the night?" Since she sensed Court had no wish to harm her, Marion was not in a hurry to return to

Camburg. Once there, they would part ways, and the stone would be locked away inside an English holding and lost to her. Until they arrived, she still had a chance.

"Aye," he said, tying his mount to a nearby tree. Though not as thick as the forest they'd passed earlier in the day, this stretch of land would provide cover.

Finished with his task, Court walked toward her. "If you run," he said, watching her intently, "you will only get yourself hurt. On the morrow—"

"I won't run," she said. "That stone you're carrying is mine. And until I have it—"

He laughed, dimples forming on both cheeks. Though he must be at least twenty and eight, Court's smile made him appear younger.

"You are laughing now, but I doubt I will amuse you later."

"You are a tenacious little lass, aren't you?"

"And you are a stubborn, arrogant boar."

He took a step closer. "You know me well, it seems."

"Your kind, aye."

Taunting her captor would not help her accomplish her goal, but it seemed she couldn't help it. Every time Marion opened her mouth, she was surprised at what came out of it. She'd never speak to her father this way, let alone any other man of rank. And yet . . . Court seemed almost pleased by her behavior.

Perhaps she shouldn't be so surprised. Her nemesis was, after all, the worst kind of man.

An Englishman.

"My kind," he said, his voice not as light as it had been earlier. "And what *kind* is that, my lady?"

"The *kind* that would steal from the most holy of persons, put a knife to an innocent maiden's throat and—"

"Innocent? Maiden?" He laughed again, and this time Marion nearly gave in to her urge to kick him.

"You are despicable."

21

Instead of responding, Court smiled. A lazy, half smile that said he didn't believe her. And with that, he turned and walked away.

After a few moments, she realized he wasn't coming back. Using the time to see to her needs, Marion continued on toward the water, where she washed herself as best she could before returning to their makeshift camp. It consisted of nothing more than a small clearing and, after she pulled it down from his saddlebag, a bedroll.

Court returned shortly after she'd begun to gather sticks into a pile for a fire. He tossed his own logs on top and proceeded to gut the hare he'd caught. Marion made a sound of disgust and turned her back.

"You prefer just to eat it then. No interest in how your meal is prepared?"

She crossed her arms and remained silent. Staring off into the darkness, she listened to his movements behind her. Just as she'd done many times before, usually when someone teased her about her "abilities," Marion contemplated how to get out of the situation with her dignity intact. She'd only turned around because she could not tolerate the sight of blood, whether it be from a hare or a man. But now she refused to look at him because he expected her to. And because she'd not admit that flaw to him.

And she'd called *him* stubborn.

"Do you plan to starve, my lady?" he mocked.

Given a cue, Marion did turn then. And gasped.

Court leaned over a fire roasting their meal. He'd removed his surcoat and chain mail. Clad in only a long linen shirt, the neckline open, and woolen hose, he looked dangerous . . . and delicious. With such a wide chest and thick arms, the Englishman could no doubt crush a man's skull with his hands, and then carry a maiden to his tent.

"See something you like?"

COURT CERTAINLY DID.

He'd had no intention of making camp this early, but every time Marion shifted, her backside brushing against him, he became more and more uncomfortable.

"Aye," she said. "Dinner."

He really should leave it at that, but something about Marion made him want to misbehave.

Walking toward the fire, she placed her hands over the flames and rubbed them together. The warm summer days often, like this one, turned into much cooler nights.

"Mmm," he murmured, her murderous glare warning him away.

At least, it would have warned off a more cautious man. Court ripped off a piece of meat and handed it to Marion as she lowered herself onto the makeshift seat he'd provided. He watched as she opened her mouth and brought it down on the roasted rabbit.

"Is it safe to have a fire?" she asked.

He concentrated on the flames rather than the redheaded beauty who was likely contemplating how to kill him in his sleep. "As safe as it can be in the borderlands."

Which meant it was not safe at all. But if they were discovered, it would not be the fire that gave them away. The little-used road would not hide their tracks, ensuring he would have a mostly sleepless night.

"So where is it?"

Court wasn't foolish enough to look down at his waist, the pocket he'd sewn into his hose to keep the stone safe. Instead, he continued to gaze into the fire. The sound of crickets was the only accompaniment to the crackling of the wood.

"Why did it call to me if I was not meant to take it?" he asked between bites, aware she would not answer him.

Marion licked her fingers. God . . . why had he looked at just that moment? "Tell me who you plan to attack and when, and I will tell you what I know of the stone."

Court pressed his lips together. He tore off another piece of meat and handed it to her. When their fingers touched, she pulled away as if she'd been burned.

A smart lass.

"I cannot give you details, but if you tell me why I was called to that place, I promise to tell you something."

When she peeked up at him, light from the fire dancing across her face, Court's sight fluttered and he had his first vision of his companion. No longer haughty, the earl's daughter was replaced with a passionate woman, lips parted and eyes hooded.

"What is it?"

He closed his eyes and waited for it to pass.

"Court?"

"A vision," he murmured, opening his eyes.

"You had a vision? Of what?"

If he dared to put to words what he'd just seen, his Scottish maiden would suffer quite a shock. Instead, he offered what he knew. Which was not much.

"I've had them my whole life," he admitted. "Sometimes years pass between them. But since the stone's pull began, I have them much more often."

"What do you envision?"

He shrugged. "I don't know. The person in front of me. But different. They seem to give me some sort of insight."

"What did you see when you looked at me?"

He didn't wish to lie to her, but he was even less eager to answer her question.

"The guard. The one with the priestess," he offered instead. "I saw him as a young boy, scared and alone."

Thankfully, she didn't continue to question him.

Placing a piece of meat daintily inside her mouth, she looked every bit the lady—her log a throne and the trees her lady's maids. He smiled as he watched her finish eating.

"These visions," she began, "are your special ability."

"My—"

"Special ability," she repeated. "Though I'm unsure exactly what it means. Mine is much simpler."

He shook his head, not understanding.

"Did no one ever explain your gift to you?"

"Gift?" He laughed. "Curse, you mean?"

She sighed. "Aye, that too."

"Nay," he said, standing. As he made his way to the saddlebag, he continued, "My mother died in childbirth. My father followed her not many years later. No one knew of my *gift*. Until now. If they had *gifts* of their own, I never knew it."

He pulled the leather waterskin from the bag and walked back to the fire.

"I fostered with Richard Caiser, Earl of—"

"Kenshire."

He wasn't surprised Marion knew of him. Though Richard had died more than two years earlier, passing the earldom to his daughter and her husband, all in the borderlands knew of the man. Some said he'd been more powerful, and certainly more beloved, than the King of England.

"Aye. He knighted me. Entrusted Camburg to me. And said nothing of my gift or ability or however you speak of it. Although I doubt he, or anyone I know, would believe such a thing."

The corners of Marion's mouth lifted in a small smile. Sympathy? Surely not. Well, he'd promised her information, and information he would give. Some.

"On a recent trip to London, Edmund of Almain ordered me to take . . ." He hesitated. "A keep." Moordon Castle had at one time merely been a keep. So this was not truly a lie.

"In Scotland?" she correctly guessed.

He nodded.

"Is this . . . Edmund of Almain one of the king's regents, then? Why would he order such a thing? Why now?"

Court had asked the man that very question. Though it was true these lands had become unstable recently, the border lines had been drawn more than thirty years earlier. The English and Scottish Wardens held monthly Days of Truce to ensure peace continued to reign between the two nations. And yet Edmund had told him it was an edict from the king himself—that Moordon would provide the foothold they needed in the event war broke out.

"He is one of Edward's regents," he answered. "While Edward continues his crusade abroad, he left his duties to two men. Any one regent would have gained too much personal power. But Edmund, along with—"

"Robert Burnell, the king's chancellor. I know some of your English politics."

He was impressed. "Aye. And as to your question of 'why now?' I do not ask, but simply follow my king's orders." For an order from the regent was the same as an order from the king himself.

That Edmund had promised him the very thing he'd always wanted, a title and land of his own, Court kept to himself. Halbury Castle was not nearly as grand as Camburg, but it would be his own.

Marion fell silent. He handed her the waterskin, and she took it. She drank deeply, her elegant neck stretched back, and then returned it to him. A lone drop of water had escaped onto her bare chest.

Don't look.

"Before meeting the priestess," Marion said finally, her tone serious, "I had no way of knowing what was true and what was legend. Growing up, the healer in my mother's village told tales of the Ladies of the Stone, women chosen throughout time to protect the stone, a symbol of Scotland herself. It was said that our lands would remain safe so long as the guardian kept the stone safe. From the priestess, I learned that if the stone fell into the hands of . . ." She looked at him with the same malice that had been directed at him earlier that day. ". . . *you* . . ."

His eyes narrowed.

". . . Scotland would be in danger. For each guardian, there is a nemesis—someone who is called to take the stone. To use it against Scotland. When the protector and her nemesis die, the stone finds its way back to the pools to be guarded by the priestess until it can be claimed once again."

"And you are that guardian?" Her tale was too fantastical to be believed. If it weren't for—

"I am."

She said it so confidently that Court froze. Her eyes held his own, never wavering.

"How could you possibly—"

"When I first told my mother of my ability to sense danger, she did not believe me, of course. It was only after many years of warnings that she and my father finally understood. And then, of course, there was the mark."

His skin tingled. "The mark?"

So it was true. Everything she told him, as much as it sounded like a jester's tale of fancy, was true.

"Do you have it?"

This time he looked down to where the strange mark had appeared just a fortnight ago. His clothes hid it from sight, but he could almost feel it burning his flesh.

"I have one as well," she said, pointing to her right hip.

Court groaned inwardly, imagining—

"Where is yours?"

He almost asked if she'd like to see it. But Court caught himself before he let the impropriety slip. Instead, he pointed to the exact same spot, but on his left hip. His mind reeled with revelations. The first thing he would do once back in Camburg was to seek out the advice of the elders. Surely there must be an English legend similar to her Scottish one. In her version, she was the protector, he the enemy. But perhaps his people had their own version of the tale.

"So you know now why you were called to the stone." She smiled sweetly. "Now you know why it is mine. I'd like it back."

4

_____

Though Court never looked down, his hand moved toward his side protectively. By all the saints, how could she steal it back if he kept it there? Her first failed escape attempt had not gone well, but this time Marion had to get it right. Once at Camburg, the stone would be lost to her forever.

"I cannot give it to you."

She'd expected him to say as much.

"But don't you see—"

"I see only what you tell me, Marion. Your version of the legend."

A shiver ran down her arms. Her name had never sounded so . . .

"It will aid my cause," he blurted out. Court tossed the bones of his meal into the fire. He looked at her, as if awaiting confirmation. The revelation seemed to surprise him even as he said it.

She'd said too much. Belatedly, Marion realized if Court had not known of the stone's importance, he may have been more inclined to give it to her. "Think first, speak later," her tutor had often said.

So much for that lesson.

"If your cause is to start a war along the border," she said, preparing to stand, "then, aye. The stone may prove useful."

"Sit," he asked. Only the softness of his tone stayed her. "We are at an impasse, it seems. But can we not put aside our differences—"

"Differences?" She shook her head, astounded. "We are enemies, Court. You aim to hurt my people—"

"Who refuse the call for peace. The border has become unstable—you know it as well as I do. Those who remember how it was before the Days of Truce say it will only get worse. Blackmail, increasing raids—"

"On both sides," she spat back.

"It would be foolish not to prepare for the worst."

She disagreed. "Surely you don't ask me to condone an attack against my own country?"

"Surely you don't ask me to disobey orders from my king?"

Marion opened her mouth and then closed it again.

What would I do in his position?

They glared at one another, Marion wanting nothing more than to reach over, grab the stone, and get away from here.

Away from him.

Not true.

She pushed away the thought, stood, and marched over to the bedroll. A thin linen blanket and makeshift pillow made from grass and leaves were to be her only protection for the night. Trying to ignore the sound of her companion moving around camp, Marion closed her eyes and breathed deeply, taking in the smell of moss and . . .

Court?

He lay behind her, pushing her over and nearly off the bedroll. Without turning, she asked, "What are you doing?"

He shifted against her, pulling the blanket over his body. It was just large enough to cover them both, but . . . did he really think to sleep this way?

"Attempting to get some rest," his deep voice answered.

"Surely not like this?" She shoved him with her backside, attempting to regain some of the space she'd lost when he lay down.

"Surely not," he answered.

Marion turned from her side to her back in order to see him. With two hands propped behind his head—at least he'd given her the pillow—he appeared quite comfortable. A man who would steal the stone, attack her country, and cause Marion to fail at her purpose in life . . . and she was drawn to him like a starving man would eye a banquet. A dangerous, virile, and attractive man. "This is not . . . proper."

He turned his head slowly, raising his eyebrows at her. "You are really concerned about propriety? After all that has happened today?"

"And they call *us* barbarians."

"Who does?"

Was he serious?

"You. The English."

Court turned onto his side, propping his head on his hand. "Have you met an Englishman before?"

"Of course." And that was the truth.

"And he dared to call you a barbarian?"

She thought about the question for a moment. "No, but—"

"I do not think that."

She tried to slow her rapidly beating heart by willing it so, but instead it did just the opposite.

"You don't?" she managed.

"No," he said, looking at her lips.

Was he going to kiss her?

"I think you are extraordinary."

It was so unexpected, Marion simply stared at him. What did she say to such a thing? That she felt the same way? That her traitorous body seemed to forget this man had stolen her destiny from her?

Foolish chit, he only thinks you're extraordinary in the way everyone else does. How could she have forgotten?

"Because of my gift," she said softly.

He didn't answer at first.

Finally, he asked, "You sense danger?"

"Of sorts." She pulled the blanket over her chest. It was getting colder with each passing moment. "I sense when someone means harm."

His jaw shifted, the slight tick a sign that he was annoyed, or perhaps anxious?

"What is it?" she asked. Court's eyes darkened. Something had upset him.

"And that is what you sense from me?" he finally asked.

She really should lie. The more information she gave him, the more power Court would have over her. "No."

They were so close that Marion could feel the rise and fall of the blanket as he breathed.

Too close.

Her answer seemed to startle him.

"Why?"

Marion wished she knew. "Mayhap it does not work on you?"

"But I saw a vision of you earlier. I saw—" He cut himself off. This time, there was no mistaking his expression. So he'd not been truthful. But he clearly didn't wish to voice the reason for his lie.

"You said your last vision was of the guard . . . Never mind," she blurted. "'Tis not important. We really should—"

"I saw your eyes hooded and lips parted, as if you'd just been thoroughly kissed."

She accidentally looked at his lips then. They were so . . . full.

"I saw the passion in you, Marion."

Oh God . . . the priestess . . . anyone. Please help me.

"But you don't know why? Or what that means?"

He shrugged, and though it appeared a casual gesture, Marion could tell it bothered him, not to understand.

Court turned from her then, muttering something about sleep.

She did the same, turning so their backsides were touching. But she would not think of that. She'd not think of where and how they touched.

No, she would not think of it at all. Certainly she would not try to imagine what his buttocks would look like—

Stop!

Marion closed her eyes against the vision, but it stubbornly refused to go away.

COURT COULD NOT TELL if she slept or not. Even if he hadn't been intent on keeping watch, he never would have been able to sleep with her so close to him.

What had initially seemed a rational decision was proving to be anything but. He'd thought he understood pain. Certainly he'd suffered the day Richard Caiser sent him away from Kenshire. And the day he'd nearly lost his arm in a battle.

But lying beside this beautiful, willful woman with the knowledge that he could never so much as touch his lips to hers . . . he would take a few battle wounds instead.

Glad they'd not encountered anyone yet today, he also knew sleep would have to elude him this night. It was simply too dangerous, with potential adversaries all around, including the one lying so peacefully next to him.

Had he been asleep, he may not have noticed her hand ever so gently lifting his shirt. He'd like to believe he would have woken, though, when those dainty fingers so nimbly pulled on the pouch that contained the treasure she sought.

Did she really think to steal the stone while he slept? And then? Did she intend to take his horse and escape alone?

He really had never met such a bold, determined woman before. It was too bad she was attempting to steal that which he couldn't give her. Part of him wanted to see what she would do next, but he couldn't risk it.

He caught her hand, grabbed it, and brought it around his chest. Rolling toward her, Marion nearly lying atop him now, Court watched her expression turn from surprise to something else.

"Trying to seduce me?"

Her face was close enough to his that Court simply had to lift his head and their lips would be touching.

"Of course not." Her green eyes flashed, annoyance mixed with the same desire he felt for her.

"Maybe you should be."

Before he thought better of it, Court lifted his head and kissed her.

Or tried to at least. It became immediately apparent she'd not been kissed properly before, so instead of pursuing his suit, Court pulled away. He very much wanted to be the one to instruct her, but with her breasts pushed against his chest and her body so dangerously close to his hardened manhood, he knew it was not a sound idea.

Regretfully, he pulled his hand away and stood.

"Go to sleep," he said, too harshly.

"Court?"

He made his way back to the fire. He tossed a log onto it and sat.

"I will not apologize for trying to take what's mine."

He looked up just as Marion had reached the center of camp. She stood above him looking . . . well . . . damned beautiful. "As I will not apologize for stealing something I wanted."

"The stone—"

"I wasn't talking of the stone."

Why was she so taken aback? Surely she had noticed he desired her.

"I propose a truce."

She sat on her own log, thankfully too far away for him to touch her.

When he looked up, her expression was completely transformed. Another vision. This time, Marion appeared crestfallen. As suddenly as it came, the vision disappeared.

She watched him, waiting. "Another vision?" she guessed.

He swallowed. "Something happened recently," he said, not knowing if it were true, unable to detect if the vision was a part of Marion's past or future. "Something that made you feel extremely sad?" he guessed.

"Likely when I learned you'd stolen the stone from the priestess."

But he was already shaking his head. "Nay, before that."

She looked down. Toward her hip. Toward the mark.

"What is it, Marion? What happened?"

Marion shook her head.

He stood and walked toward her. He bent down, the desire to comfort her overwhelming.

"I didn't want it to be true." She spoke so quietly, it took Court a moment to realize what she said.

"The calling," he guessed. Though her head was still bent, he could see her eyes close briefly. A blessing . . . and a curse. The thing that made her special, or so she believed.

And he had claimed it.

Court lifted her chin, forcing her to look at him.

"The truce? If you'll have it still."

Even frowning, Marion was extraordinarily beautiful. He couldn't believe what he was about to say, and yet the words left his lips nonetheless. "You can have it."

God, he was a fool.

"The stone," he clarified. "It's yours—"

Marion wrapped her arms around him so quickly, the movement nearly toppled them both. As good as she felt so close to him, he pushed her away, not wanting her to misunderstand. "After the attack. I need it to carry out my orders. Then the stone is yours."

She sank back down as he continued.

"You can stay at Camburg until it is over. And then you may take it back to Scotland."

Scowling, as angry now as she had been happy a moment ago, she said, "Very well."

He propped his hands on his knees, still squatting in front of her. "Will you tell me what the vision was about?"

"It was that morning." She looked down at her concealed mark again. "The day it appeared."

"Your parents must have been—"

"Proud." She laughed—a hollow, empty sound that reminded him of the vision. "They were proud, and excited, and a bit nervous too."

"Then why—"

"I did nothing to deserve it."

When she looked into his eyes, Court saw himself. Hadn't he always questioned whether he deserved Richard Caiser's sponsorship? The opportunities that had landed in his lap?

"They were not proud of me. This gift . . . I can't control it. It's just like my ability to sense malintent . . ."

Though she stopped, Court could understand all too well. This was why he felt a burning need to prove himself, to show everyone, once and for all, he deserved the opportunities he'd been given.

He could have told her she was special for much more than her gifts, that he'd never met a woman like her. That he wanted nothing more than to press his lips to hers and lose himself trying to fulfill his earlier vision. Instead, he stood, reached out his hand, which she took, and guided her back to their bed in the forest.

Once they were lying down again, he lifted the blanket over them and said, "This time, do try to keep your hands off me."

He smiled when she chuckled, but his merriment was short-lived. As she moved into a comfortable position, Court prepared for a long, long night ahead.

5

She awoke nestled in Court's arms, a feeling so unusual that her first instinct was to scramble away. Her second was to move closer, which was exactly what she did until his pained moan from behind stopped her. The sound sent a rush of feeling through Marion. Of all the men her father had presented to her as possible husbands, none had ever made her skin tingle and her heart beat as quickly as this Englishman.

This Englishman who was now pulling himself away from her.

"Not yet," she heard herself saying. "I'm cold."

She was no such thing. The heat from his body fended off the crisp morning chill just fine. But when Court wrapped his thick arm around her shoulder once again, she sighed and moved closer to his warmth.

They had lain that way for what seemed like hours, though only a few moments had passed, when a familiar feeling came over her. But this was not the slight chill that had warned her of danger before. It was as if she'd stepped out into the coldest of winter days. So cold it hurt as she sucked in her breath.

"Marion?"

Court must have sensed it too, for one moment she was

contemplating the wisdom of her hastily uttered command for him to stay, the next, she was lying on her back, Court peering over her, his eyes wide and brows wrinkled.

"Danger," she managed to say, watching Court jump to his feet, sword immediately in hand. The bitter cold lessened, though it did not go away completely. Marion rubbed her arms to warm herself, coming up behind Court.

"My dagger."

He spared her the briefest of glances before walking toward his horse and pulling the weapon from where it had been hidden among his belongings. Handing it to her silently, he looked in both directions, and when she nodded toward the north, Court motioned for her to move around him.

When she did, he untied his horse, his movements quick and silent, and pointed to the stirrup. Marion let him assist her in mounting, and as she silently grabbed the reins, still holding her dagger, he whispered to her, "Stay here. If you see anyone but me approach, ride away as fast as you can."

After pausing to be sure no sounds reached them, Marion whispered back, "I will not leave you."

"You can, and you will."

With that, he strode toward the ridge that hid them from view but also concealed whatever enemies neared them. Marion looked up to the sky, the sun finally having made an appearance, and waited.

I will not leave you.

It was as if her words had forgotten to reconcile themselves before escaping her mouth. She should have said, *I will not leave the stone.*

Court moved toward her so silently that she didn't notice his approach until he was nearly upon her. He mounted behind her and spurred the horse to a slow canter. She wanted to ask what he'd seen, but they sped up before she could speak. And as she had the day before, Marion silently admired his horsemanship. They navigated the terrain effortlessly, and only when he finally slowed again did she ask what had happened.

"A gang of reivers," he replied.

"How many?"

"At least ten."

She didn't ask if they were English or Scottish because it didn't matter. A reiver's allegiance was to clan and family first. Ten of them riding together could only mean one thing—a raid. Besides, had not she felt their intent?

He navigated off the main road and onto a path marked more by overgrowth than evidence of other travelers. "I'd hoped to be at Camburg by nightfall, but we'll be lucky not to have to make camp again now."

"Will my men be there before us?"

"More than likely, aye."

They rode at a more reasonable pace, Marion's backside beginning to ache from the brutal pace they'd set the day before.

"That could have been . . . interesting," Court said.

Marion had just been wondering what would have happened had her ability not given them advanced warning.

"You said you've had this—gift—for many years?"

"Aye, though never like that before. The cold . . ." She shivered thinking about it.

"Is it the stone, then?" he asked. "Does it make the sensations stronger?"

Marion thought back to what the priestess had told her—precious little, and nothing of her ability. "I'm not sure," she said. "There's much I still do not know. Just that when I'm close to you . . . to it . . . I feel at peace. After the mark appeared, I felt unsettled, as if something were missing."

"I felt the same."

A noise startled her, but when she saw the movement in a bush just ahead, Marion realized it was an animal of some kind.

"Are you scared?" His voice was like the blanket he'd pulled over her last eve. Comforting and warm. The voice of her enemy, but he felt less like one with each passing moment.

"Nay," she said honestly. Oddly, she had never felt truly scared of him, with the exception of the moment he'd held his sword to her throat. But even then . . . Marion should have been terrified—freezing—but she'd had no premonition of coming danger. Was it the stone that prevented her from sensing a threat from Court? Or could it be that he did not pose a threat at all?

Impossible.

So long as he held the stone and intended an attack on Scotland, he posed a very real danger, indeed.

"Where do you intend to attack?"

"You know I cannot tell you that."

"When?" she tried again.

"Marion . . ."

"Then why?"

"That you already know. I've been ordered—"

"To do so. But that does not answer my question."

As they rode through an open field, the marshland giving way to rockier and slightly steeper terrain, Marion decided she would learn everything she could about her English knight in order to convince him to relinquish the stone before his planned attack.

"Do you always follow orders?"

"Of course," he said, without hesitating.

"Even if it hurts others?"

He hesitated. "In war—"

"But we are not in war, Court. We are at peace. Our countries—"

"Peace," he spat. "What do you believe those men back there intended? To break their fast with us?"

"Reiving is a way of life along the border."

"And stealing cattle or sheep is one thing. Murdering innocents, quite another. Surely you know the borderlands become more dangerous with each passing day? Bribery abounds, mistrust threatens to rip apart the tenuous peace."

She turned to peek at him. "An attack will most certainly help matters, then."

Court's eyes narrowed and he slowed until they were at a complete stop.

"What do you want from me, Marion? You want me to call off the attack? Tell the king's regent I refuse to follow his orders on the request of a beautiful Scottish woman I met while on my way back from the pools? The very same place I was called to find after a mark appeared on my hip one morning, one that apparently signifies I am the nemesis of the protector of Scotland?"

She turned her body as much as was possible in the saddle they shared. Though his words mocked, Marion heard something behind them that gave her hope.

He did not want this attack any more than she did.

"Do you believe it is the right thing to do?"

He continued to glare at her.

"Would you do it if—"

"Nay." His hard tone was directed at himself, and not her. She would not let him intimidate her.

"And your overlord? Geoffrey and Sara of Kenshire, do they believe—"

"Nay," he said again. "Is that what you want to hear?"

"I just want the truth. Nothing more."

"The truth?"

Court's eyes darkened and dipped to gaze at her lips. When he looked back up, Marion's heart began to thud so loudly it was a wonder he couldn't hear it.

He dismounted and helped her do the same. Without looking at her, Court moved his horse off the road. He tied their mount and walked back toward her.

"The truth is that I want you, Marion. More than I've ever wanted any woman before. Though you'd sooner slit my throat than come willingly to me, it hardly seems to matter. I'm drawn to you as surely as I am to the stone."

I want him to kiss me.

"That is not true."

"I am not drawn to you?" He took a step closer. So close she could smell the mint he'd chewed earlier that morn.

"Nay, that I would sooner slit your throat than come willingly to you." A dangerous statement, but a true one nonetheless.

"Do not," he said, shaking his head. "Do not give me permission."

This time, it was she who took a step toward him. It made little sense, but Marion would have plenty of time to rue her actions later. For now, she'd speak from the heart.

"I want you to kiss me," she said, proud of her bold proclamation.

For a moment, it appeared as if he would do it, but instead, Court looked away. She'd been a fool to say such a thing. Marion turned from her adversary and walked away.

COURT WATCHED her go from the corner of his eye. It was for the best. Nothing good would come of giving into that which could not be. There were too many reasons not to kiss her.

She was a noblewoman and therefore a virgin. The exact kind of woman he had done well to avoid all these years. Even if it were not for the fact that she claimed they were mortal enemies . . .

Dammit.

Court reached her in a few strides. He grabbed her arm, spun her around, and pulled her toward him in one swift motion. When she parted her lips just before he lowered his own, Court's body immediately responded, and he reminded himself to slow down.

His tongue showed her how to respond, and she did, opening her mouth almost immediately. Court took full advantage, his tongue capturing hers as his mouth slanted to the side for greater access. When her arms wrapped around him, Court pulled her closer.

She learned quickly, and soon the kiss spiraled deeper into a descent that would be hard to pull out of. He could not get enough of her. Court was desperate to tear off the travel-worn gown and touch every inch of skin beneath. In anticipation, his hands moved to her cheeks, wanting to come into contact with her smooth skin. He guided her, kissed her, and nearly lost himself to the sweetness that was Lady Marion of Ormonde.

Pulling away from her took every bit as much strength as lifting a broadsword for the very first time. Only his honor—and the horror of disrespecting her—gave him the ability to do so. Her lips, swollen from his kiss, were slightly parted. Her eyes, wide and bright, just as they'd been in his vision.

"My apologies," he said, taking a step back.

"But I asked you to do it. What are you sorry for?"

Indeed, what?

"That we had to stop."

Her look told him he hadn't needed to stop at all. The reivers had obviously taken the main road or they'd have caught up with them before now. Only his honor had forced them apart at this moment.

"You don't know what you ask for," he said, realizing the truth of his words. Marion's dazed expression told him as much. This was likely the first time she'd been thoroughly kissed. Experience told him where a kiss like that would lead, so it was his duty to stop it.

By God, he'd wanted anything but.

"We need to go," he said before he changed his mind. Her expression closed down at once, and she merely nodded.

It was only hours later, when they stopped for a brief respite, that either of them spoke again.

"You're hungry?" he asked, already knowing the answer. They'd eaten little, but if they continued to push on, he and Marion could still get to Camburg that night. They'd passed the only other keep between the border and Camburg Castle, an abandoned pele tower that was once fortified by Clan MacAdder, a clan no longer. This close to the border, only those with strong alliances and plenty of men behind them could survive.

"Aye," she said, walking back toward him from where she'd seen to her needs behind a thicket of bushes.

"If we stop now, I fear—"

"I can wait."

She raised her chin. But Court finally recognized the gesture for what it was—not haughtiness but pride.

"You are a remarkable woman," he said honestly, wondering if she knew it.

"My ability is—"

"Nay." He walked toward her. "I don't speak of your ability but of you. For someone who has been sheltered much of her life . . ." He shook his head, not trusting himself to finish.

"You are not bad either . . . for an Englishman."

He couldn't help but smile. "High praise from the Protector of the Stone."

Damn. Why had he reminded them both of their situation?

She didn't look angry. Instead, she crossed her arms in front of her. "So are you the Man of the Stone, then?"

He wished he knew.

"I am nothing. Just a simple knight following orders."

When she continued to watch him, Court's heart picked up its pace. It was as if she tried to look beyond his words. As if she could see *him*.

"Tell me something of Richard Caiser," she said as she walked back toward the horse and mounted for the last time. He raised himself up behind her, prepared for another torturous ride with Marion so close he could feel her, smell her . . . Without the mail and surcoat he'd left behind that morning escaping the reivers, precious little separated them, which would make this day an even more difficult one than the last.

"He was the most honorable man I'd ever known."

Court told her of how he came to squire for Richard Caiser. Of his childhood at Kenshire and of his desire to please the man who'd felt like another father.

"You speak little of the daughter."

With good reason.

"Sara and I were . . . are . . . quite close."

"What is she like?"

He conjured her in his mind, the girl who'd become a woman right before his eyes.

"She is like you in many ways," he said, realizing the truth of his words. "Strong-willed and resilient. She'd have been a great warrior if she had been born a man."

"You don't believe a woman could be a great warrior?"

Court imagined Sara in the boys' breeches she'd worn so often when they were growing up. In fact, the last time he'd visited Kenshire, the countess greeted him dressed that way.

"I don't doubt one could," he amended. "But few are trained for it."

Then he remembered the dagger he'd taken from Marion yesterday. The one she wore on her hip even now.

"You know how to use that," he said, patting her hip and wishing he had not.

"I do," she said. "Though a dagger is of little enough help when a great oak is holding a sword to your throat."

"A great oak?"

"Your arm," she said as the sun began to fade away. "I've never seen an arm so thick and . . ."

Unfortunately, she stopped. Court would very much like to know what she would have said next.

"I am sorry for that," he said finally. "I'm sorry for all of it. Marion, if I could give you the stone right now, I would. I do not want to cause you any further pain or distress."

She didn't answer, but her back, so stiff and straight yesterday, leaned casually against his chest. At least part of her trusted him, a boon he hardly deserved. He gently pulled her head toward his shoulder, and she accepted his invitation. Shifting a bit, she found a comfortable position and settled against him. Court resisted the impulse to lean down and kiss her head. Instead, he lifted his chin and stared ahead. Waiting and watching until it finally came into view ahead in the darkness.

Camburg Castle.

6

*A*t first Marion didn't know where she was. Waking abruptly, she sat up in a large, canopied bed and looked at the light streaming through the one lonely arrow slit above her. She jumped from the bed and made her way toward the door. Nearly stumbling on something, Marion looked down and almost squealed with delight. How had her belongings come to be here?

A knock at the door had her running back to the bed. Lucky thing since the maid who entered the room was followed by four young male servants carrying . . . a tub! Pulling the coverlet over her, Marion watched as they carried it to the center of the room.

"My lord thought you'd be wanting a bath, my lady."

The maid, a girl of no more than ten and nine, stooped to open Marion's bag. Pulling out the nicest of the two dresses Marion had brought along, the maid held it high in the air.

"'Tis lovely," she said, and Marion silently agreed. She'd planned on wearing this dress for her first meeting with the priestess. Though it was sturdy enough for riding, its crimson coloring and gold inlays caught the eye. But when Marion had spied the mountain they were to climb to reach the pools, she'd decided against wearing it. It was, after all, not a banquet, and though more practical than most, the gown was still unsuitable for her purpose that day.

But judging from what she'd seen of Camburg Castle last eve, it would do well here. She had been given the impression Camburg was a modest estate, but the sprawling square fortress was anything but. Had she asked after her men? Everything was hazy after Court shook her awake on his mount, but the memories of last eve slowly came back to her. Her men had not yet been spotted.

"Your other gown is being washed, my lady," the girl said.

"What is your name?" she asked the maid as she watched the servants carry buckets of deliciously hot water into the chamber.

"Elaine," the girl replied, nimbly preparing her gown. By the time the tub was filled and Elaine handed her a large piece of lavender soap, Marion forgot everything. Her quest for the stone, her longing for the man who should be her enemy. All of it fell away as she closed her eyes and reveled in the thought of clean skin. She had not had a true bath in more than a fortnight, and the pleasure of the prospect was akin to . . .

Nay! She'd not think of that kiss.

But of course she would. It had occupied her thoughts ever since. At first the passion and intensity had startled her, but her surprise had melted away. She'd not once thought to stop him, for her body ached for the very thing he offered. Though it was wrong for too many reasons to count, his lips had felt—

"My lady?"

She focused on the maid, who handed her a drying cloth.

Turning her attention to getting dressed, Marion rushed to dry her hair and get into the gown. The sooner she could get dressed, the sooner she could eat.

The only time Marion had been this hungry before was the night of the banquet her father had commissioned in her honor.

Excited, she'd entered the hall at Ormonde only to realize he'd intended for the banquet to pressure her into choosing a suitor. When Marion saw all the young men seated in their hall, she'd decided not to eat that night, or the following day, out of protest. She'd been quite young, and foolish.

As she dressed, Marion learned that Elaine had joined her aunt and uncle at Camburg the year before, after both of her parents were killed in a raid. A familiar tale along the border, and one Marion was accustomed to hearing from her own people. But in their stories, it was the English who destroyed families and were to blame for their current troubles.

Belatedly, she realized Elaine did not seem bothered that she was Scottish. She would certainly not remind her of the fact now.

As soon as Marion was dressed, Elaine escorted her down a long corridor and down a winding stairwell. The great hall was bright and well decorated, filled with red and yellow striped banners and fine tapestries. Ten trestle tables were lined up, set for the morning meal. And as she entered the room, every single one of the men and women sitting at them turned to stare.

That was the reception she'd expected.

She paused and stared back, but she found her eyes drawn to the far end of the hall. How could she have missed him earlier?

Court stood and walked around the high table toward her. He looked nothing like he had the day before. The growth on his cheeks gone, his hair freshly washed. Clad in a fine surcoat of black and gold, Court looked every bit the lord.

By the time he reached her, all eyes were on them. Bowing, Court extended his hand. When she took it, the same feeling came over her as when she'd awoken in his arms the day before.

The mad notion that she never wanted him to let go.

"Well met, my lady." He guided her toward the high table.

"Good morn to you, my lord," she responded formally.

When they sat, it was just the two of them.

"Do you have no visiting nobles?" she asked. The high table at home was nearly always full. Her father had always been fond of entertaining despite the danger that lurked just outside their castle walls.

"Just one," he said, pushing his trencher toward her with a wink.

Eventually, the others went back to their meal, though Marion caught a couple of men and women glancing at her covertly, eyes narrowed, as if she were the enemy.

Which, of course, she was.

"Camburg's hall is . . ." She looked up at its wooden beams and around to the whitewashed walls. ". . . splendid." And she meant it.

"Richard adored this castle," he said. His tone was warm, as it always was when he spoke of his former mentor. "When he put me in charge of it, I was truly shocked. At the time, it was one of many properties he owned, but with the exception of Kenshire, I believe it was his favorite."

"At the time?" She picked up a piece of bread and ate without reserve.

"Sara has since given many of the Caisers' holdings back to the crown."

She was about to ask why when he continued.

"To appease Lord Lyonsford"—he looked sideways at her —"the man to whom she was betrothed."

"Betrothed?"

Court frowned. "When she fell in love with her husband, Geoffrey, she was betrothed to the Earl of Archbald."

Marion's hand froze halfway to her mouth. Something about how he said her name . . . her husband's name . . . "You are in love with her."

He did not appear pleased about her observation.

She was right!

"*Was* in love with her," he finally corrected. "I care for her, of course, but she is married now."

Marion thought back to what he'd said before. And while she

51

filled her stomach, she pieced together that which he had not told her.

She had an idea of what may have happened. "Richard gave you Camburg to get you away from Kenshire. Away from his daughter."

Court's face twisted in a way that told her she was right.

"But why? You said he loved you like a son. That he—"

"He did." Court scowled at the cheese on their trencher as if it had gone bad.

"So why did he—"

"Richard had plans for her. Bigger plans than a young knight with nothing but an ancient title and no land to go with it."

The pain in her chest came without warning. And the strangest thing about it was that Marion could not tell if it was sympathy for a man who had been deemed an inferior match for the woman he loved, or the knowledge that he had loved that woman so deeply that it continued to affect him.

Either way, it did not concern her.

The stone. She had to remember her purpose here.

"I'm sorry," she murmured, finishing her meal.

They continued to sit in silence until the hall began to empty.

"I've been away," he said finally, "and need to meet with my men. As soon as yours arrive, I will send for you."

Her plan. She needed to get that stone before he attacked Scotland.

"And I may walk the grounds, speak to people here?"

He looked at her oddly. "You are not a prisoner here, Marion. You may leave at any time. When your men arrive—"

"Nay," she said, much too quickly. "We have an agreement."

"One I mean to honor."

He stood, and she did the same. "Elaine can show you—"

"I will find my way," she assured him.

"Very well," he said with a slight bow. "Until we meet again."

He walked so quickly from the hall, Marion wondered if perhaps she'd offended him. The thought pained her, but in the end, it hardly mattered. She needed to learn all she could about her Englishman. And either convince him to relent on the attack or get him to let his guard down enough for her to take what was hers.

She meant to have the stone. She meant to do her duty as its guardian.

WHILE HE SHOULD HAVE BEEN PREPARING for one of the most important battles of his life, Court found himself pacing the ramparts of the castle Richard had entrusted to him so many years ago. Even a brutal training session could not get visions of him and Marion together out of his mind.

So many strange things had happened to him over the last few weeks, from the appearance of the mark to the pull of the stone. But none had taken him more by surprise than his feelings for Marion.

It was more than desire. He'd known that from the moment she walked into the great hall that morning. The sight of her had nearly poleaxed him in the gut.

Forget Marion. Victory is within reach.

Almain had promised him Halbury Castle just to the east of Camburg. Moreover, he'd hinted that he would arrange an advantageous match for Court once he completed this mission.

Forcing his mind back to the upcoming battle, Court envisioned Moordon Castle, an ancient keep once held by the English. The castle had fallen into disrepair after a raid more than ten years ago, which had forced the English owners back south. He knew not who currently held it—it could be any number of Scottish nobles and clan chiefs, from MacAdder to Douglas as the new owners. It hardly mattered. His scouts had confirmed the king's regent's assessment of the situation. Moordon existed on a skeleton staff, and its strategic location was ideal for the raids that may be necessary if—or when—war broke out once again along the borders.

And yet . . . he found himself thinking of what Marion had said. Sara and Geoffrey certainly wouldn't approve of his actions. And such a measure was as likely to cause a war as to stave one off. And while once appealing, the thought of a titled bride no longer appealed.

Do not be foolish.

Defying the king's regent, losing a potential stronghold . . . he simply could not do it.

The sun had set long ago, but Court could not bring himself to attend the evening meal. He should not force Marion to eat among strangers, but seeing her again in that shape-hugging gown, the epitome of nobility and grace . . .

Skipping the meal was the right thing, for both their sakes.

Court descended the stone stairwell and strode through the square courtyard lit only by torches along each outside wall. He navigated the large well in the center of it all and made his way into the main keep.

Damn. The hall was still filled with retainers and servants alike. Avoiding the entranceway, he made his way along a long corridor and nodded to the guard at the top of a winding stairwell that led to the lord's chambers. Was he a coward for evading her? Aye, but a coward who knew his own weaknesses, and Marion was one of them.

He pushed open the door of the chamber and was about to pull it closed behind him when a voice stopped him.

"Court?"

Oh God, no. Not here.

He turned, reluctantly, and instantly regretted it. The desire to reach for her—to touch her—was almost impossible to ignore. He wanted to smooth out the line of worry between her brows, make her smile. Or better yet, flush with pleasure.

Marion looked confused. He didn't blame her.

"My lady," he said, trying not to look at the expanse of creamy skin her gown revealed.

"I thought to speak with you at dinner. I'm worried for my men."

He was as well. They should have arrived before them, which was why Court had sent three of his own men north to see what they could discover. Oddly, he did not want her to know that. The thought of her knowing that he cared should not bother him. But it did.

"I'm sure they are well," he said. "And will be along anytime."

Her frown indicated she did not agree, but Marion inclined her head in parting and began to walk away.

Lord watch over him, he was about to make a bad decision. A very, very bad decision.

He reached out and pulled her back to him and inside the chamber. With one hand, he closed the heavy oak door, and with the other, he reached up to pull her face toward his own. Capturing her lips, Court branded her with a searing kiss.

She kissed him back with such wild abandon Court was left breathless when he pulled away to look at her.

"This cannot end well," he said, warning himself as much as her.

"I agree," she said, her arms wrapped around her shoulders.

"I will not stop the attack," he said softly, knowing the words might push her away. Half of him wanted them to; the other half wanted this moment to last forever.

"I am a virgin," she said, "and must remain such for my husband."

It was as if she'd doused him with water from the River Esk, frigid even now during the summer. "Husband?"

Was she betrothed, then? To whom?

55

"The man I will marry," she said, looking at him as if he'd gone daft.

Court backed away as if burned. "Who?"

She stared at him blankly.

"When?"

Understanding finally dawned, and Marion lifted her chin, a sure sign he was about to receive a tongue-lashing.

"I am betrothed to no one," she said. "I just meant . . . it is one of the many, many reasons I should not be alone with you in your bedchamber now."

She is not betrothed.

And what in God's bones was wrong with him? Would it have made a difference if she were?

Aye. It would have mattered. When he touched Marion . . . even when he simply looked at her . . . one thought ran through his head: *mine.*

He took a step back toward her and captured her neck from behind. "We have established that this is foolish and wrong. But by God, Marion, I've never wanted anything in my life more than I want to kiss you again. To tear off that gown of yours and cherish what lies beneath it."

To make you mine in truth.

When he brought her head toward him this time, the kiss was gentler. While their tongues tousled, Court finally allowed himself to explore the maddening desire that she'd awakened in him.

Dipping his hand beneath the fabric of her neckline, he reached lower until his hand was able to cup the round, beautiful breast below. Taking it firmly in his grasp, Court teased her nipple with his thumb as he continued to show Marion with his mouth how deeply he needed her. When she moaned beneath him, a kitten-like purr that instantly hardened his cock, he released her breast and prepared to replace his hand with his mouth.

Trailing kisses from her mouth downward, he shoved the fabric on her shoulder aside and continued his exploration. He didn't dare open his eyes. The sight of her breast beneath his mouth might crack his already-thin resolve to leave his Scottish noblewoman a virgin this night. But by the time his mouth finally reached her hardened nipple, Court was not sure how long that resolve would last anyway.

Marion grasped his hair at the back of his head and pulled him closer. He met her demands, nipping and squeezing, showing her exactly how much pleasure she could expect from him that night.

When Court finally backed up and gazed into her wide, clear green eyes, he felt an unmistakable tug on his heart.

"We cannot continue," he said.

Marion licked her lips. If she did that again, there would be no turning back.

"I've never felt like this," she said, her honesty so endearing that Court couldn't decide if he wanted to ravish her or protect her for all eternity.

"There's something between us, Marion. If it were not for the stone, for your position—"

"My position?"

He stepped back and ran his hands through his hair.

"You are an earl's daughter. And I—"

"You believe *that* is the biggest problem between us?"

The moment was gone. Thankfully. Marion righted her gown and crossed her arms. His feisty Scottish lass had returned.

"That . . . and the stone."

"Nay." She shook her head. "Not the stone. Your stubborn refusal to see what is in front of you. The 'peace' you talk of so fondly is about to be ripped to pieces by the very person who claims to cherish it."

"I have no choice," he ground out, tired of this argument. Tired of fighting with her. With himself.

"You always have a choice."

With that, she pushed against him, ripped open the door, and left.

A good thing, because Court had nearly made the biggest mistake of his life.

7

*H*e had nearly taken her virginity.

Four days later, Court climbed the stairs that led to Camburg's round hall. Named by the lord who'd once ruled here, a man with no heirs who'd allowed the castle to revert back to the crown, the round hall was nothing more than a circular chamber atop the east tower. The four windows gave him the best —and most well-lit—view in the castle. Staring out of one shuttered window, Court could see as far away as the small village they'd skirted on their way back from Scotland. Beyond that and slightly to the north, he could see the land that would become his once Moordon was captured.

He would continue to hold Camburg for Kenshire, but he could finally begin a life of his own rather than one loaned to him. One that did not include a blasted stone and a redheaded woman who tormented his thoughts every moment—waking and sleeping. Or her prickly guards who had arrived two days earlier, along with the men he'd sent to find them.

Court pushed his surcoat aside and reached down into the pouch he carried at all times. Pulling on the gold chain, he lifted the emerald stone and laid it out on his hand. This simple stone was responsible for all that had transpired since he awoke with the mark. Without it, he never would have met Marion.

Turning it over in his hand, Court felt nothing out of the ordinary. And after speaking to the elders of Camburg over the past few days, he was no closer to learning more about his own role in Marion's legend.

Sounds filtered to him. Court tightened his grip, hiding the stone from view as the door creaked open.

"Marion."

The sight of her took his breath away, affecting him as potently as if he'd not avoided her for days. The green overtunic above her cream-colored kirtle matched her eyes.

"'Tis a wonder you remember my name." She closed the door behind her, looking around the room. Using the candle she'd brought with her, she proceeded to light each of the three wall torches.

"I hadn't noticed the dark before. 'Tis usually quite light in here."

She placed the candle on the small table beside them.

The nearness of her was almost unbearable. *This* was why he'd been taking meals in his solar. Why he'd been meeting and training, leaving Marion to explore. Why he'd been unable to sleep. Unable to think straight. Unable to do much of anything except wonder what it would be like to give in to temptation. To toss Marion onto his bed and spend an entire night pleasuring her.

"You've been avoiding me."

There was no use denying it.

"We need to talk, Court."

For one wild moment, he envisioned himself laying waste to the contents of the table before them, clearing it to make way for Marion's luscious body.

"Court?"

He had to get out of here.

"I can't—" He tried to move past her, but this time it was she who stopped him.

"Please."

Her hand branded him, the linen shirt not enough of a barrier against the heat of her touch.

"I need to know how long we'll be here," she pressed. "How long until—"

"One more week." He could no longer deny her. Not when she stood so close, not when she was touching him. He turned as her hand fell. "One more week and I will be gone. Afterward, the stone is—"

"Gone where?"

"Marion, please." It was his turn to beg.

"I know about Halbury Castle."

Light flickered across her skin, illuminating her faint freckles as well as her eyes, which reflected every bit of the judgment he deserved.

"And?" he said, his voice harsh.

"That is why you are intent on this mission. Not because you are 'following orders.'"

If she had approached him with caution, it was gone now.

"Not because Almain is the king's regent."

Kissing her was not the only way to stop her from saying it aloud, but it was one way. And so he kissed her with every bit of the pent-up desire he'd felt over the past few days. His body was immediately engulfed in a raging battle, one he was not certain he'd win.

One he didn't want to win.

WHEN HIS LIPS TOUCHED HERS, Marion cursed herself for a fool. She'd intended to confront him about his planned attack, not to end up in his arms again. But the passion they shared for each other had changed her, and she found it difficult to go back to playing the earl's innocent daughter. She was not the woman who'd set out on a quest to become the next protector of Scotland. She was a woman who understood desire, who could recognize the fluttering deep within her body for what it was. One who, despite her best intentions, would not stop this dangerous course.

With every flick of their dueling tongues, Marion was pulled deeper and deeper into an irreversible decision. One that would infuriate her parents, change her future, and bind her to the man she'd sworn to overcome. Despite the implications of lying with a man that was not to be her husband, Marion could not seem to pull herself away.

When his mouth moved from her lips to her neck, Marion tossed her head back to give him greater access. Since her arms could not fully encircle his broad chest and shoulders, she did the best she could, gripping his tunic and clinging to him lest her legs give out under her.

"So sweet," he murmured against her neck.

She'd come here to confront him about the attack.

Not for this.

At least, that was the story she told herself. But the way her body responded, the things he made her feel . . . some of her, maybe all of her, had hoped their last kiss would lead to more.

When he abruptly pulled away, the loss was immediate. One moment, his hands and lips were on her . . . the next, he crossed the room toward the door.

He locked it.

Her heart skipped a beat.

Turning, Court stood by the door and simply watched her. She took in his tunic, opened wide at the collar allowing for a peek beneath. His expression was predatory and male, one that sent a shiver down her spine.

She thought he would say something then, but instead he moved to the table at the center of the room, swept its contents off with one swipe of his arm. A ledger went flying to the ground, and before Marion could see its final destination, Court was in front of her. He picked her up easily and carried her to the edge of the table. When he positioned her in front of him, she could feel the most intimate part of him pressed against her stomach.

He lowered his head once more, both hands gripping the back of her head, as if she needed encouragement. Every thrust of his tongue, movement of his hips, made her want more. She returned his kiss greedily.

"Something . . . ," she tried to say. But how could she describe this new pressure in her core? This tingling deep within her that longed to be set free?

He tore his lips from hers and looked into her eyes. Ever so slowly, his hand moved back down until it reached the hem of her kirtle. Lifting both it and the undertunic up at once, Court closed his eyes. A primitive sound escaped him as soon as his hand found her bare flesh. Still looking into her eyes, he pushed aside each barrier until he reached the part of her no one else had ever touched.

Marion should have been embarrassed enough to break eye contact, to turn away. She held his gaze instead, mesmerized by the dance of his fingers on her skin.

"What are you doing?"

Court's only answer was a slow, sensual smile that made her insides pulse. His smile deepened as he slid his fingers inside her. With his free hand, he opened her leg as he pressed and withdrew, circling and flicking his fingers.

Marion was lost.

Gripping each side of the wooden table, she resisted the urge to close her eyes, wanting to see his face, wanting to watch his expression as it changed from pleasure to . . . something else. No longer smiling, Court looked at her with an intensity she recognized. This was what he'd looked like the day she'd warned him about the reivers. Determined, resolved. But this time, the only threat was that she'd lose her heart to the enemy.

"I've imagined doing this every night since waking with you pressed against me."

Marion tried to breathe.

Court lifted his chin, his hand pumping faster now. "And this is just a taste."

The intensity of his gaze, the intimacy of his fingers inside her, she wanted to hold on to this moment forever. But Marion simply couldn't. She did close her eyes then, pushing her hips toward the delicious sensations that were building and building . . .

"Come for me, sweet Marion."

A pulsing sensation at her very core gripped her like a violent wave, turning her around and around so that she couldn't tell up from down. Squeezing the table, trying to catch her breath, Marion finally found her way. Now the sensations were like an ebb and flow, still pleasurable but not threatening to drown her.

When she opened her eyes, Court seemed quite pleased with himself. He licked his lips, leaving a trail of wetness behind.

"Don't do that," she said, unable to look away from his wicked lips.

When he raised an eyebrow rakishly, Marion knew she'd said the wrong thing. This time, his movement was deliberate. His tongue not only darted out, but it captured the lip below. She simply could not look away.

"You shouldn't have told me you liked it."

She reached up to one of his biceps and squeezed, giving in to another one of her curiosities. He was as hard as the table she sat on.

"Who said I liked it?" she teased, not wanting their easy banter to end.

"You did ask me to stop."

"And I also asked you not to attack my people," she said, aware her words would ruin the moment, but unable to stop herself. "But you did not reconsider."

"A discussion for another day."

"Another day? When the attack is imminent?"

He looked as if he'd argue with her. Instead, he took a step back and held out his hand to assist her off the table. "Tomorrow?"

He stood so close that Marion could feel the heat of his body.

"You'll not disappear on me again?"

Court lifted his hand and laid it on her cheek. For a man so large, his touch was surprisingly gentle. "I don't make promises that I do not intend to keep."

You've made none to me.

But it was better than nothing. "Aye," she agreed. "I look forward to it."

Unfortunately for her, she looked forward to more than just their discussion.

8

"*A*ll is ready, my lord."

Court's captain and most trusted advisor, who had been with him since he left Kenshire, bowed as he began to leave.

"Shall I send in the Scot?"

Court nodded. The leader of Marion's small band of men, Kenneth, had requested an early audience with him. He entered the solar chamber and did not waste time on a greeting.

"How much longer must we stay here?"

"I don't believe, sir, that is any of your concern."

"I have been charged with—"

Court stood and took a step forward. "With following your lady's orders. And she told you, quite clearly, you are to remain at Camburg for a fortnight, at least. And await further orders."

Kenneth scowled. "I cannot stand by with my lady a prisoner—"

"Prisoner? Is that what she told you?" He knew she'd said nothing of the sort to her man. It was obvious he simply did not trust her judgment, which for some reason infuriated him.

"Not precisely, but—"

"But you think to take control of a woman you serve, one who clearly has the intelligence to carry out her duties."

The look Kenneth gave him was so full of contempt he had no doubt the man would have attacked him had it furthered his cause.

"I suggest," Court said when Kenneth turned to leave, "you speak to Lady Marion if you have further concerns."

He left and Court sank back into his seat. Before parting from Marion last eve, he'd promised to find her before his training session. It was time to do just that, but she wasn't going to like what he had to say.

Delaying, Court thought about the evening before. The raging need to be inside her, claim her, the uncontrollable urge to be the first to show Marion what could come of the passion that he'd awoken in her. It couldn't be, no matter how much he wanted it. The attack, the stone . . . if only their circumstances had been different.

It was for the best that the attack would be over soon. If all went well, he'd be gone less than one week. And then he could give her the stone and return to his normal world. One of his own choosing. Though not, unfortunately, one which included Marion.

He rose and after a brief search found her in the great hall . . . playing chess?

"Your move, my lady."

A young knight named Marcus sat across from her. And though the hour was still early, the men's training not yet begun for the day, Court nearly ordered the knight out of the hall. Marcus looked at Marion the way any man would regard such a beautiful woman. Unbidden, a vision of Marion in the round tower, her head back, hair streaming all around her, assaulted him.

"You wished to speak to me?"

67

Both she and Marcus startled at his tone. Sensing his displeasure, the knight scrambled to his feet and left them alone. Or as alone as they could be in a crowded great hall.

"Only if you can manage a civil conversation, my lord?"

He was tempted to say that he could not.

"Come."

Without waiting for her, angry at himself for his reaction to a simple game of chess, Court led her out of the hall and down a secret passageway. Descending a few stone stairs, he opened a door, which led to—

"A garden!"

None used this path but he. Shielded from the rest of the herb and flower garden, this patch of greenery and the small courtyard surrounding it was a rare private space. One he wanted to share with Marion.

"'Tis lovely," she said, her hands gliding across the coralbells as she walked.

It is you who are lovely.

"Why are you so cross with me this morn?"

Not prepared for the question, Court scowled in answer. "I am not—"

"Aye," she cut in. "You are."

She wore the same riding gown, now laundered, as when they'd first met. Her hair, no longer flowing freely, was clasped back on both sides, a simple twist holding the remainder in place.

He couldn't very well tell her the truth about his ill-considered jealousy. Instead, he broached another equally delicate topic.

"I know you hope that I may reconsider the attack—"

"But you will not," she finished for him.

"My orders—"

"What would happen if you did not follow these orders?"

She asked too much of him.

"I would suffer. Kenshire would suffer. You yourself could not answer what you might do in the same circumstance. Not to mention Almain could . . ." He stopped. What would the regent do exactly?

"But you would suffer most of all. Without your precious Halbury, you would not have your land and title." Her chest rose and fell with indignation.

"You think that's all I care about?"

"Am I wrong?"

Court shook his head. "You'd never understand."

"Try me."

He knew she'd do anything, say anything to stop this attack, and yet he found himself opening himself to her nonetheless. "I loved her," he said. *Stop, Court. Don't make a fool of yourself.*

But if he didn't, she would push and push, and either he'd succumb or he would be forced to ignore her until she had the stone. But he'd tried that, and it didn't work.

Marion was not a woman to be ignored.

"Lady Sara," he said, the words like acid in his mouth. "But I was not enough. Richard loved me, cared for me, but he never intended me for his daughter."

"But you are a knight, a lord—"

"A title given to me by Richard."

"Surely he—"

"Knew what I did not yet understand. I was foolish, but after this raid—"

"You will be the very same man I stand before now."

"No," he said. "You're wrong. I will be the man who was generously rewarded for obeying the king's regent. Land, title, an advantageous marriage."

She pursed her lips. "So that is why you've waited, even though Lady Sara has long since married."

"Waited?"

"I wondered why someone like you was not already wed."

"Someone like me?" The edge was gone from his voice, and he sounded weak, plaintive. He should have never opened his mouth.

"Someone strong and protective. A champion for the weak, one who is disciplined, if not a bit arrogant, and who clearly knows how to please a woman."

She took a step closer to him.

"You please me well, Sir William, Lord of Camburg."

An instant jolt of lust was followed by an ache in his chest that felt as if it would tear him apart. He had not asked for those words.

"Don't, Marion."

She took yet another step toward him.

"Why?" she asked.

The answer was too painful. He longed to be with her, but he could not go through it all again. Even without having to answer to Almain . . . even if she wanted them to be together, her father certainly would not. It was easier for him to turn the conversation back to her.

"What of you? As the daughter of an earl, you must have had enough marriage proposals to be wedded and bedded thrice over by now."

"Wedded, nay. Bedded . . ." She shrugged her shoulders.

She deliberately goaded him.

Court reached for her and pulled her toward him. "You have not—"

"And what if I had?"

The thought of Marion lying with another man . . . "No."

Her scowl was fierce and instantaneous. "You've no claim on me to say such a thing."

"And yet I'll say it just the same."

When he brought his lips down on hers, neither of them softened the impact. The kiss was rough and uncompromising. Court reached for her back, her hips, and brought her even closer, showing her the evidence of his words.

"I want that claim," he said, gasping as he pulled away.

She didn't even hesitate.

"Then it is yours."

AFTER AN ETERNITY, Marion finally gathered enough strength to pull away. She could not think with Court's lips on her own. This was the second time she'd come to speak to him of the attack—and ended up in his arms instead.

Trust the stone.

Court was not the enemy. He could be if she didn't stop him, but the same stone that had given Marion her ability had been guiding her all along. They were not enemies. Court meant no ill toward her, or even to her country. Not truly. If he had, she would have sensed it. He only thought to follow orders—in part because he wanted that which he already had. He simply hadn't realized it yet. He may have been given Camburg, but even that had been earned. Court was already a man to be admired. There was nothing left to prove.

Court still held her shoulders. "You don't know what you're saying."

He looked terrified. Understandably so.

His expression softened. "Marion, I—"

A brief knock landed on the door, and it then swung open.

"My lord. A visitor has been spotted approaching the gates."

Marion looked at Court as the many possibilities ran through her mind.

"Who?" Court demanded, his eyes locked with hers.

"The king's regent," the guard said with more than a tinge of fear in his voice.

"Edmund of Almain."

The man nodded his acknowledgement and then turned to leave. "Aye, my lord."

The implications of her failure to convince Court to abandon the attack finally began to penetrate.

And now it was too late.

9

What was Almain doing here? This was not part of the plan. Court's mind raced as they walked toward the hall together.

Then it is yours. The only thing more surprising than Marion's declaration was his own. He *did* want that claim.

"We don't have much time," he said, pulling Marion into an alcove just before the hall's entrance. "There are only two ways a man can claim a woman. And neither of those are acceptable for us. I spoke rashly—"

Marion reached out and took his hands. The familiar gesture nearly tore Court in half.

"As did I," she said. "But how can we deny there is . . . some-thing . . . between us?"

"Mayhap that something is the stone," he said. "A connection forged because of it." It was a thought that had entered his mind on the sleepless nights he'd spent away from her.

When he looked down to where it lay, her gaze followed.

"May I?" she asked.

He could not deny her. He disengaged one hand and took the stone from its pouch, pulling the gold chain upward so that the emerald green shone and spun. He handed it to her. While passing it, a strange jolt coursed through his body. Judging from her expression, she had felt it too.

"It belongs with me," she said.

You belong with me.

With the chain still wrapped around her delicate fingers, Marion reached for his hand once again. When they joined hands this time, the chain between them, Court saw a glimpse of the two of them in this same pose. They wore different clothes, however, and Marion's expression was one of contentment, not concern. The vision left him as quickly as it had come.

"You've had another vision," she guessed correctly.

"Aye," he said, unable to bring himself to describe it to her. He could not allow himself to hope. How could they have a future together when Edmund's decree stood between them?

If he attacked Moordon, he would lose her. If he didn't, he would lose everything he'd worked to achieve. And perhaps his head along with it.

Court leaned toward her, and when her eyes closed, he was nearly felled by the trust she put in him. He didn't deserve it. But he kissed her anyway. When her mouth opened for him and her tongue hesitantly explored his mouth, he pressed himself against her. Wanting to be closer, to feel all of her. The need to be inside this woman was so strong that Court vowed it would happen. She would be his, one way or another.

He broke the kiss and stood back, taking the stone with him. "Come," he said.

"What will you do?"

An agreement had passed between them, one he had initiated. But how that agreement reconciled with his mission, Court could not begin to contemplate.

"We must go," he said, turning. He had no answers yet.

"We?"

Marion followed him into the great hall, where his guest was due to arrive at any moment. Perhaps Edmund could be convinced of another way, but he didn't dare voice such a hope to Marion. For if it didn't work . . .

"Stay with them." Court gestured to the men who stood on both sides of the entrance.

Marion, who was clearly no less confused than he was by his inclusion of her, stood to the side. He walked toward the high table and took a seat in his usual place, opposite the chair that had been positioned in front of it. Court nearly laughed at Marion's attempt to mesh with the others. She might as well be dancing in the middle of the hall. She was like a lone white cloud in a sea of blue, evident from every direction to all who chanced to look. Beautiful and untouchable but certainly noticeable.

They didn't have to wait long. Court heard Almain's retainers before he could see them. As they streamed into his hall, he counted no less than thirty men.

When Almain entered, Court stood and waited as the short, beady-eyed earl made his approach. Bowing as the man came closer, he silently rued that he should have to be subservient to a man who had never served in battle, never once bloodied his own hands.

"Well met, my lord," he said, straightening.

Rather than respond, Almain looked around the hall with an assessing gaze.

"You do well by Camburg," he said.

"To honor the memory of Richard, I would do anything," Court said. And meant it.

"The girl and her husband are lucky to have you."

Lady Sara was no girl, and he was the lucky one to have their support. But Court remained silent. Almain was both older and, if the rumors were true, crueler than the new king. He was not a man to be trifled with.

"You must be tired from your journey," he said, still unsure why that journey had been made. "Would you like—"

"What I would like," Almain said, "is to know when Moordon Castle will be ours."

NAY, it could not be!

Moordon Castle? It had no men to speak of—certainly not enough to pose a threat to Camburg, or England—and it would have long since fallen into disrepair if it weren't for her father.

Did Court know it was theirs? Is that why he'd refused to reveal the location to her?

When Court's guest had walked into the hall, a chill had coursed through her at once, so powerful it had nearly brought her to the ground. Certainly her ability had grown stronger since the mark had appeared and she'd first come into contact with the stone. But this was . . . indescribable. When the English earl had walked by her, she'd struggled even to stand. Marion had no doubt this man intended to do harm. To her? To her country?

And then the man had mentioned Moordon, and thankfully, she began to feel herself once more. Because she would have to act, and quickly. Her own cousin had been sent to Moordon when the king granted it to her father asking for him only to restore the ancient holding to its former glory. But why the regent would want—

Its position.

Moordon was not valuable, but its position at the threshold of strategic holdings was very much so. Did this mean Edward would break the thirty-year truce? Did he intend to wage open war with Scotland once again?

"Your Grace, I believe we should discuss—"

"Discuss?" Almain spat out, his contempt for Court's words apparent.

Marion's hands began to shake as she watched the proceedings. How could she have so completely misjudged him? She'd nearly given herself to a man who would attack her own people . . . What had she been thinking?

You were not.

She'd allowed the man who'd stolen the stone to edge his way into her heart. In doing so, she'd failed to fulfill her destiny. Marion had failed miserably at the one thing she was supposed to do well.

"Well," Almain pressed. "When do you attack? I've brought some of my own men to ensure victory. You still want Halbury, do you not? And an heiress to go with it?"

Court's eyes met hers.

"Of course, Your Grace."

The traitorous English bastard. The son of Satan. How could she have trusted him? Listened to him?

Fallen in love with him?

He could keep the damned stone. Marion had to warn her people.

She fled the room, running as quickly as her feet would carry her, out of the hall and into the courtyard. How could she have been so utterly foolish? She should have . . . what? Stolen the stone? Court was too intelligent to have allowed that to happen. Seduced him first and then stolen it? Injured him and taken it by force?

She chided herself even as the thought crossed her mind. But certainly the worst thing she could have done was wait around for him, trusting him and believing, even for a moment, that he'd begun to care more for her than his own ambitions.

Fool. You are a fool.

"Pardon," she said to one of the gatehouse guards. Trying to keep her voice calm, she inquired after her men.

"They are just above," a young knight, mayhap even a squire, said. He disappeared and emerged a short time later.

"What's wrong?" Kenneth said.

They didn't have much time. Moordon needed to be warned.

"We must leave," she said. "Now."

Without waiting for an answer, Marion rushed across the courtyard to the stables. She would find out soon if Court had been lying about her status here. Guest or captive?

"My men and I are leaving," she said to the stable master just inside the entrance.

Kenneth caught up to her as their horses were being readied.

"What is happening?" he demanded in his typical condescending tone.

She was having none of it. She would treat the man who protected her with his life with the respect he deserved if he could give her that same courtesy. If he could not, she didn't need him.

"Kenneth," she said, "that is quite enough. I will remind you that I am the daughter of Archibald Rosehaugh, 3rd Earl of Ormonde, and the Protector of the Stone of Scotland. You will either speak to me with the same respect you give my father, or any other man of status for that matter, or you may remain here, relieved of your duties to me and my family."

The other men arrived during her speech. The stable master and one of his hands gawked at them openly, and Marion couldn't blame them. By the time she finished, her voice likely carried back into the hall, where Court and the king's regent plotted her people's demise.

"Aye, my lady," he said. They stared at each other a moment longer, a new understanding dawning between them.

"Circumstances have changed, and we need to leave. Now."

Kenneth's eyes widened and he opened his mouth but promptly closed it. Instead, he gave her a quick nod and turned to the others.

"You heard the lady. Let's go."

Marion would have smiled had the situation not been so dire. In a flurry of activity, she and the men prepared to leave Camburg.

I may have failed to retrieve the stone, but I will not fail Moordon.

As she rode away from the stable and through the courtyard, Marion wondered why Court had allowed her to leave. Though she looked over her shoulder, once, twice, as they rode through the gatehouse and beyond, there was no sign of pursuit. Nothing.

And just like that, the stone, and the man to whom she'd inadvertently given her heart, were gone forever. She ignored the pull that tried to lure her back. The stone would not protect Moordon now.

She would.

10

*C*ourt watched as his unwanted guest was led from the hall.

He had to find Marion to explain. When she'd dashed out of the hall, Court had very nearly run after her. But he'd reminded himself of her words, her pledge, and trusted she would understand. Whatever happened next, they would be in it together.

He should have questioned Almain's motives earlier. But he'd been too stubborn, too blinded by his own ambition to see what was before his eyes. The stone had revealed the truth to him— everything had become clear as he spoke to the king's regent.

A vision had nearly knocked him off his feet. In front of his very eyes, Edmund of Almain had transformed from an elegant agent of the crown to a snarling, vindictive man. The man's eyes had narrowed as he looked at Court in greedy anticipation of the spoils at Moordon. As the vision peeled away, Court fully understood the ability the stone gave him for the first time.

He could see things as they truly were. Or in some cases, how they would be.

He wasn't sure how he knew, but Edmund's intentions were not honorable. Was it because Scotland would suffer or was it more than that? Either way, he had to find out. He also needed to speak with Marion, but first he would need to find her. It was only after he searched her rooms that Court's pulse began to race.

She wouldn't have left, not after everything they'd shared. Would she have?

Every step he took toward the stables brought him closer to the truth. Marion was nowhere to be found because she had left. Did she have so little faith in him? He'd agreed to Almain's plan for one reason—he needed to pacify him until he had an alternate plan. But had he ever told Marion he wouldn't make the attack? What precisely had he said to her?

A connection forged because of it.

Nay. That was not true. There was so much more than simply the stone between them. So why had he said it?

Because it was easier than facing the truth. Court had fallen in love with a woman who circumstance dictated was his enemy. One who likely despised him now.

Damn, Court. What have you done?

He needed to go after her, but he could not do that. Not yet. One of the most powerful men in all of England, powerful enough that he had been chosen as a regent to Edward, would be returning belowstairs for dinner, and Court needed a plan before then.

Preparations for the meal were already underway. What the hell was he supposed to do now? Almain expected him to lead an attack he was not prepared to conduct. He strode to a table where a handful of Almain's men sat. Court had to be careful, but he recognized one of them and could hopefully get information from him.

"Sir Roger, son of Lord Wellingstone?"

Lord Wellingstone was an honorable man, one who fought on the side of peace at the border. He assumed the son was no less.

The man looked up at him as conversation ceased around him.

"The same," the heavily bearded man replied.

"You serve Almain now?"

"Until my knight service ends, aye."

Almain's men would never betray him. To do so would risk the wrath of a man who could wreak havoc on their lives. That meant Court could not be direct in his line of questioning, but he didn't need to be direct to discern if his suspicions were correct.

"And will you take Moordon with us?" he asked, keeping his eyes on the man's face.

The look that passed over Sir Roger's face—and the visages of his companions—told Court that none of them were particularly pleased about this particular mission.

"We will," he said only.

Court had his answer.

"Enjoy the meal and the hospitality of Camburg." He inclined his head to the others. "Good day, sirs."

With that, his course of action firm, Court waited for his guest to arrive. Ignoring the activity around him, he sat. And drank. Waiting for his future to be decided.

Unfortunately, a certain redheaded vixen distracted him from the task at hand. Instead, he saw her waking up beside him, felt her soft flesh beneath his hands.

"I want that claim."

"Then it is yours."

No matter what happened between them, or to him, Court did this for her.

And for the borderlands.

He had one hope. Robert Burnell, the king's chancellor and co-regent of England, was the only man who could challenge Almain and the only person to whom Court could appeal if he hoped to refuse Almain's request but keep his head.

When Almain finally reappeared and was escorted to the high table, Court did not wait for him to be seated. He'd finish this now.

"Before you sit, Your Grace," he said, not quieting his voice or caring who heard them. "I would know one thing."

The man's mask of confidence slipped. "Which is?"

"Does this attack have Burnell's full support?"

It was a guess. A wild guess at that. But with the cloud of his own ambitions lifted, Court could see so much more clearly.

And one glance at Almain told him his suspicions were once again right.

"What is this?" Almain's voice was tinged with anger, and perhaps a bit of fear as well.

"I asked if this attack on Moordon has the support of Robert Burnell."

"Listen to me well," Almain spat, "I am regent to Edward I, King of England, and you are nothing. Certainly no one to be questioning me. You will take Moordon Castle or see yourself locked in the Tower."

He'd expected the threat.

"For?"

"Treason. Disobeying direct orders from your king." Almain, furious, turned to look at his men. Though he'd brought several of them, Court had many more retainers who were already present. The man turned back to Court. "You will pay for this display. As will Kenshire."

He could endure threats to himself, but Court would not allow one against Geoffrey and Sara. They had naught to do with his foolishness, and they would not suffer for it, even if he did. "If it is peace you want, I will give it. My allies at the border will quell this unrest and uphold the Treaty of York. Is that not truly the goal?"

By speaking openly, he backed Almain into a corner. A very dangerous proposition, especially given the man's open show of temper, but the only one he had.

"That will not happen," Almain snapped. "When Moordon grows stronger, and it will, the Scots will push back into our own borders. They'll have the foothold they need to destroy us."

"Nay, they will not."

Everyone, including Almain, turned to look at the entrance of the hall where Marion stood tall and proud, engaging with a man who could summon England to war with her own country if he so desired. Even this far from her, Marion's voice was clear and strong.

God, she was magnificent. And judging from Almain's expression, very much in trouble.

SHE'D ARRIVED JUST in time.

Marion walked toward Court, trying to appear unaffected by the icy waves of air emanating from the man who stood at the back of his hall as if he owned both it and all of England. She'd learned from Court's confidence, and if there was ever a time to appear confident, it was now.

"I don't believe we've had the pleasure of an introduction," Almain said, making clear with his tone how very displeased he was with her interruption.

Court obliged. "Meet Lady Marion Rosehaugh, daughter of the 3rd Earl of Ormonde—"

"And Moordon," she said, adding her father's most recent acquisition to his title. She arrived at Court's side and, turning to face Almain, continued, "I am also the betrothed of Lord Thornhurst, seneschal of Camburg Castle." She did not dare look at Court. "So I can assure you, my father will not declare war against his daughter's husband. Or any of his southern neighbors."

Almain's face turned a dreadful shade of purple and red at her declaration, but she forged ahead anyway. "He is very much committed to the thirty-year treaty, to the Days of Truce, and to peace along the border. Enough so to ensure its success with this marriage."

Marion did chance a look at her supposed future husband. His expression impressed her—he looked nothing like a man who had just learned about his own betrothal.

"Why . . . ," Almain sputtered. "You said you were prepared to attack," he finally managed, enraged.

"I could not understand why you insisted on this raid," Court pressed him. "It took some time for me to realize that your concern is for your own interests, not for England," he told him boldly. "But as you can see, there's no reason to pose this attack. Marion's father is—"

"I know who Ormonde is," Almain spat out.

The regent wanted to punish Court. A new chill ran up her back. This man intended to hurt the people she loved and, if allowed, would strike at the very heart of the treaty that had allowed some modicum of peace in the borderlands these last few decades.

When she felt Court's hand, Marion thought he was attempting to interlace his fingers with hers until she felt the chain.

The stone.

She took his hand then, and together they held the stone. In that moment, any vestiges of cold were gone, replaced with the exact opposite. A warmth so consuming it felt as if she and Court had ventured outside to stand under the bright summer sun. She wasn't sure if Court felt it too.

Almain stared at them, wide-eyed, and then turned to look at the men gathered in the hall. Marion had not noticed earlier, but Court's men looked as if they were prepared to fight at any moment. None had unsheathed their swords, but they were clearly ready to commit treason for their lord. For if they did strike down Almain or any of his men, it would be akin to an attack on the king himself.

Even so, Almain would be taking a great risk if he punished her love. He would be declaring, once and for all, that he was an enemy of peace.

The tension hung in the air for a long moment, and then without warning, Almain's chin rose and he addressed Court very differently than he had before. "Very good, Thornhurst. You've done well to avoid bloodshed and secure the western border." He nodded to them both. "Congratulations on your impending nuptials."

Marion thought carefully about her next words and decided to forge ahead.

"I do believe Halbury would suffice as a wedding gift."

For a moment, she thought perhaps she'd pushed too far. But when Almain threw his hands up in the air as if granting a wish, she smiled for the first time since entering the hall.

"Of course, of course. Thornhurst," he said to Court, "Halbury is yours."

Almain's men looked at him as if he'd gone mad, but she sensed no rush of cold from them. They had not brought any malintent to Court's hall. They'd only gone along with their leader.

"We shall stay to celebrate."

With that, he walked around the dais to the side where she and Court stood and sat next to Court as if he'd not threatened him moments earlier.

Would they really sit and eat with this man as if nothing had happened? It appeared so. But Marion was afraid to let go of the stone. What if it was controlling Almain's behavior? What if he reversed his position as soon as they released it?

Court finally decided for them, letting the stone fall into her hand as he pulled away. She looked at him as he walked around to the other side of the table. Following, Marion sat alongside him and caught Kenneth's glance. He had not known she would declare herself betrothed to Court. She had not known herself. But oddly, he did not look surprised. She smiled, hoping to reassure him and the others that all would be well. After the day she'd put them through, they were owed an explanation. And she would give it to them.

After she and Court had the opportunity to talk about what had transpired. And whether or not they were indeed going to become man and wife.

11

They must have appeared to Almain like any other couple, but he and Marion were anything but. She played the part well, smiling and laughing as if she'd not just set down one of the most powerful men in England. Court wasn't sure what to think of her performance, aside from being grateful for her timely entrance. But he needed to know her mind.

Now.

"If you will excuse us," he said, at the risk of further insulting Almain by being the first to leave. "I must escort my lady to her room. You will, of course, be shown to yours when you are ready to retire."

Almain lifted his goblet, a signal that his wine was not yet empty. "A splendid night to you both," he said, looking at his men. "I shall speak with you about Halbury in the morning before we depart."

Court escorted Marion from the hall then, pausing only briefly so she could have a word with her men. She took his arm as she followed him down a darkened passageway and up a spiral staircase.

"My bedchamber is not this way, my lord," she said beside him, her voice like a gentle breeze on a cool summer night.

"I know well where it is."

She followed in silence until they reached his destination. Opening the studded door that led to his own chamber and adjoining solar, Court gestured for her to enter. She did, and he was pleased to see his room had already been prepared for the night. Candlelight glowed from every corner of the room. Though large, it was sparsely furnished with only a bed, two chairs and a hearth, which was not needed on a warm day such as this one. Court needed little, though he aspired to much. And yet . . . now that he'd achieved that which he'd always wanted, his own castle and lands, he found the victory a hollow one. The only thing he cared about was the woman standing so close he could reach out and touch her.

But he did not.

If he laid a hand on Marion, they'd not have the conversation they so desperately needed to have.

"You came back," he said, unsure of where to begin.

"I did."

He couldn't do this. Court gestured for her to sit in one of the chairs, far enough that he could not reach her.

Once seated, Marion opened her hand and revealed the stone, entangled in the gold chain to which it was attached.

"Did you feel it?"

"Aye," he said. "It felt like I was seeing everything as it should be even without a vision. What happened?"

Marion looked down at the stone in her hand. "I do not know. From what I've learned, the stone has only ever been in the hands of the protector or the protector's nemesis, not both at the same time."

When she looked up, Court nearly lost his resolve not to touch her. She was so very lovely.

"I thought you'd betrayed me," she said.

He had assumed as much—and decided he couldn't really blame her. If she'd mistrusted him, he was to blame. "So why did you return?"

She looked at him with such intensity the hairs on his arm rose.

"I felt his malintent," she said, "when he walked into the hall. I should have known then that he was purposefully deceiving you, but you agreed to the attack so readily, and I was too angry to consider it logically. It was only after I calmed down that I reconsidered."

"Moordon is truly your father's?" He still could not believe it. He'd never heard of a greater coincidence, and yet mayhap it was not surprising at all given everything else that had transpired between them.

"It was recently bequeathed to him, aye. I thought for certain you knew that, at first, but then . . ." She shrugged. "I took a chance."

She had put everything on the line for him, and he knew it. He had done the same for her in the end.

"Marion," he began. "I'd not betray you. Now or ever. I don't pretend to understand the power of the stone, but I'm grateful to it for bringing us together."

Her smile touched his very soul. "I've never announced my betrothal to a roomful of witnesses before."

Court stood.

"If you meant what you said in the hall"—he reached out his hand—"I would be honored to have you as my lady wife."

She laid the stone down on the seat below her and took his hand, allowing him to help her to her feet. "I wasn't sure if—"

He couldn't wait any longer. Court leaned forward and captured her mouth with his own. She responded immediately, and before long, the kiss turned from one of a shared declaration to something much, much more.

This beautiful, incredibly astute woman who'd walked into his life only a week before was going to be his wife. And he couldn't wait any longer to make her his in truth. When he slipped his hand under the hem of her kirtle on both sides and pulled upward, she did not protest. Neither did she say a word when he did the same to her undertunic.

Standing before him in nothing more than a shift, Marion peered at him, waiting.

He discarded his surcoat and tunic more quickly than he'd ever disrobed in his life. When her eyes lowered to his bare chest, Court's cock responded immediately. When she reached out a tentative hand, Court captured it and placed it on his chest. Willing himself to take it slow, he watched her explore. She traced the lines of muscle in his stomach, and then the little minx actually trailed her fingers even lower.

"It is not always this way," she said, referring to his straining cock. Only a layer of hose separated her delicate touch from the evidence of his need.

He sucked in a breath. "Nay, it is not."

His eyes rose to hers, and what he saw there nearly brought Court to his knees. He'd wanted to go slowly, but it was just not possible. Lifting her up in his arms, Court carried her to the bed.

"You are sure about this, my lady?"

Laying her down, he then stripped the only remaining barrier between them save her shift. As he awaited her answer, Court stood beside the bed completely naked. Her gaze was not shy. His body responded to the mere suggestion in her eyes that she was indeed sure about what they were about to do.

"Very sure," she said, as if reading his thoughts.

He knelt beside her, lifting her shift up as she wiggled to allow the soft fabric to glide off her body. She slid it over her head, and he sucked in a breath at the sight of her round, firm breasts.

Then his gaze moved down to her hip, and he spied the small, dagger-like mark shaped exactly like his own. When she noticed where he looked, Marion stared at his own mark. After a moment, he was roused from his momentary fascination by one much more grounded in this world. He cupped her beautiful breasts as he studied her face, then lowered his head and took a small taste. Allowing one hand to wander between her legs, he used his tongue to taunt and tease her nipple until his hand finally found its mark. Already wet and ready for him, Marion gasped when he entered her with his fingers. Her reaction changed his plans. He'd bring her pleasure more than once this eve.

He lifted his head to watch her, and when she arched her back toward him and closed her eyes, Court whispered words of encouragement.

"I will please you well this night," he said as she began to find her first release. "And every night after it."

When the throbbing subsided, he reluctantly withdrew, moving atop her and replacing his fingers with the tip of his manhood. He throbbed, wanting nothing more than to be inside this woman, to claim her as his own. A rush of heat coursed through him as she gripped his arms, her passion answering his.

When her breathing returned to normal, he said, "If I do this, you will be my wife."

In response, she thrust her hips toward him, forcing him to guide himself deeper, to break through her maidenhood. Marion let out a gasp of pain and began to pull back.

"Nay," he said, moving his hands to both sides to support himself as he lowered atop her. Capturing her lips, slowly, passionately, he used his tongue to make her forget the temporary pain. When she began to move again under him, Court knew she was ready.

He started slowly and then circled his hips until she was moving with him.

"Oh God, Court I cannot . . ."

"You can," he said, willing her to feel as much pleasure as he did. He couldn't hold on much longer. The luscious body he'd imagined under him writhed and moved with him as if she'd done it many times before.

But she had not. Marion had never been with a man before, and he would be her first and last. The thought filled him with contentment, her moans the most beautiful sound he'd ever heard.

"Thank you," he said, watching her.

Marion's eyes flew open. "For what?"

"For choosing me." He pressed himself into her and moved in a way that he knew would help her find fulfillment. Sure enough, Marion cried out, the telltale throbbing his signal to let go. His release was so powerful that he met her cries with one of his own. Utterly spent, he collapsed on top of her, making sure his elbows were propped enough not to cause her discomfort.

They lay there like that until Marion twisted beneath him. Moving to her side, Court closed his eyes while he returned from whatever other world he'd journeyed to just then.

"Court?"

When his breathing slowed, he opened his eyes once again and turned his head. The sight of her, thoroughly ravished and looking more than a mite content, stirred his cock awake once more.

"Aye?"

"I enjoyed that very much."

He trailed his finger from her shoulder down to her breast and continued exploring the soft curves of her stomach, her waist, her hips. By God, if it truly was the stone that had brought him this perfect woman, then he would worship it all the days of his life.

"I'm glad to hear it," he said, "as we will be doing it often."

She turned then, propped her head on her elbow, and smiled. "I wonder if it's ever happened this way? If the stone has ever brought both protectors together in this way."

"Ah, so now I am a protector too?"

93

When she reached out her hand and laid it on his cheek, Court's chest ached with a very new emotion.

"I did not believe so at first—"

"When I held a sword to your throat?" he asked ruefully.

She mimicked his earlier motion and let her finger fall from his face downward, toward his manhood. A shiver that had nothing to do with cold ran through him.

"I never felt cold near you. I should have known—"

"How were you to know I would love you . . . protect you and hold you dear for all the days of my life?"

When her eyes widened, he knew the words had penetrated. Just to be sure, he repeated them, only this time he added, "I love you, Marion."

In response, she looked down at his growing cock and then back up to meet his eyes. He laughed at her brazenness and pulled her atop him.

"And I love you. All of you," she teased.

Before he made love to her again, he would ensure she understood their position.

Lifting her hair to one side and placing it behind her ear, he reached up and held her beautiful face in his hands.

"If for some reason your father does not condone the match, we will run away. You are mine, Marion, from this day forward. And I am yours just the same."

When she licked her lips, he knew their discussion was at an end.

"If that is true"—she shifted her position to better prepare for what was to come next—"then I do believe I'd like to make love to you again."

Court was more than happy to oblige.

EPILOGUE

Halbury Castle, England

"My lord, my lady." The steward approached them just as Marion and Court were preparing to sit for the midday meal. "A visitor has arrived and asks to speak with you both."

Marion looked at her husband, wondering if he'd seen anything unusual. His visions came fairly regularly now that they were in possession of the stone, but she had not felt a premonition of malintent since encountering Lord Almain. Since they'd married and moved to Halbury Castle, none had threatened them, and her power had thankfully lain dormant.

A visitor was nothing unusual, so why did their steward behave so oddly?

"Show them in," Court said.

"She asks for a private reception."

Marion and Court exchanged glances. Though others may not have seen it, Marion glimpsed a slight crease in his forehead. If he was worried, then she was as well.

"Who is she?"

"She gave no name. But she—"

"Show her to the east tower chamber," Marion said, anxious to see who could inspire such wariness in the steward. If her parents had not just returned to Scotland after a brief visit to Halbury Castle, she would have expected they were the visitors. Marion smiled, remembering her parents' reaction—their joy that she and Court had found each other.

Suddenly, Marion knew the identity of their visitor. At least, she suspected she did.

By the time she and Court made their way to the visitor, she was convinced the Priestess of the Stone would be inside the private chamber to which she'd been shown. Marion squeezed her husband's hand and received a reassuring squeeze in return.

She was about to share her thoughts when they turned the corner and were greeted by a guard. Marion was still learning the layout of her new home and had not realized they were so close.

Court nodded to the knight standing at the door, and when they entered the room, Marion held her breath, waiting for the cold to come. But it did not, *would* not, for she had been correct. Would the priestess be angry at their decision? A familiar face smiled at them as they entered. It was strange to see her here, in this very ordinary room. The pools suited the priestess much more than this chamber.

"I apologize for the request," she started as soon as they walked into the room. "I cannot stay long."

Her lilting voice filled the chamber, and she smiled as she glanced down at their still-joined hands. Relief washed through Marion. She did not appear to be upset.

"I came to see if that rumor was indeed true."

Marion and Court exchanged a glance.

"This"—she waved a hand toward them—"has happened only once before."

Surprised, Marion asked one of many questions she had about their joining and the stone.

"I wondered about that, but how is it possible? We thought the stone might be responsible for bringing us together."

The priestess gave Court a stern glance. "Nay," she said. "Your seizure of the stone ensured only that Lady Marion would find you."

"Does that mean—" Court began.

"Your joining has nothing to do with the stone." The priestess looked at Marion then. "May I see it?"

"How did you—"

"I can sense it, as you can."

Marion let go of Court's hand and reached into the small leather purse hanging at her side. Pulling the stone out, she began to hand it to the priestess, but the ethereal woman shook her head.

"Nay, it is yours now." She looked at Court. "Both of yours. I keep it safe only when it awaits a new protector. At least"—she frowned at Court once again—"my ancestors and I usually are able to keep it safe. To see things as they truly are . . . that is a power I've never encountered before."

Marion squeezed Court's hand. No doubt he was confused, as she was, but it seemed unlikely the priestess would ever reveal how she'd known about their powers.

"But now that it is in your possession, you will protect it, together."

"What is my role?" Court asked. He'd asked Marion's mother what she knew about the stone and his role in protecting it, but she'd had no answers for him beyond what she had already shared with Marion.

"That stone," the priestess said as Marion put it back where it belonged, "is the lifeblood of Scotland. Most often, its nemesis intends harm upon our land. But now our interests are aligned with those of our southern neighbors. It is possible that the borderlands will suffer without your joint protection. And with it, the fate of both Scotland and England."

They were to protect the border. And peace along the border meant peace for their two lands. Of course.

"You came all the way here just to ensure the stone was safe?" Marion asked.

When the priestess smiled, a warmth filled the room.

"Your love, your union, and the power the stone has given you will guide you. May you both find joy in each other and in your protection of the stone."

With that, the priestess made her way around them, and as quickly as she had come, the woman was gone.

"I did not even say farewell," Marion said finally.

Court pulled her toward him, wrapping her up in his arms. "That was an . . . interesting . . . visit."

"Aye, very much so. At least we have some answers."

"And, more importantly . . . privacy." Court's hand ventured from her waist to her backside, and when he squeezed gently and pulled her even closer, Marion knew they would not be eating for some time.

When he kissed her, her heart raced as if it were the very first time. So it was not the stone after all. They'd been brought together by something much more powerful.

"I love you," she murmured.

"And I love you," he said. "Do you believe me?"

She startled. "What kind of question is that? Of course I do."

Court frowned in mock sadness. "Ah, well that is a shame."

She pulled back and looked up at him.

"If you had not, I was prepared to prove it."

He was insatiable.

"In that case," she said, sliding her hand between them. "I'm not sure I do believe
you."

His slow, sensual smile confirmed that the meal would indeed have to wait.

"Then by all means, let me show you."

She looked forward to the lesson and hoped it would be repeated today and every day for the rest of their lives.

THANK you for reading THE PROTECTOR'S PROMISE. I hope you enjoyed reading about Court and Marion.

DON'T MISS the next book in the Border Series, THE ROGUE'S REDEMPTION, coming in October. Become a CM Insider for release news and more Border Series goodness.

IF YOU WANT the notice but not the free prequel and other bonuses that come with being a CM Insider, follow me on BookBub for a new release notice only.

LOVE the Border Series and being on the inside? Join the Border Ambassadors, a private reader group on Facebook, for even more deSowlis goodness.

LAST BUT NOT LEAST, if you're also a fan of vampire romance with an origin story tied to the Border Series, sign up for the CM Insider- Vampire Edition.

~CECELIA

BECOME AN INSIDER

The best part of writing is building a relationship with readers. Become a CM Insider to receive a FREE copy of *The Ward's Bride: Border Series Prequel Novella* and a bonus chapter of *The Thief's Countess*. The CM Insider is also filled with new release information including exclusive cover reveals and giveaways with links to live videos and private Facebook groups so I can get to know my readers a bit more.

CeceliaMecca.com/Insider

ALSO BY CECELIA MECCA

The Border Series

ABOUT THE AUTHOR

Cecelia Mecca is the author of medieval romance, including the Border Series, and sometimes wishes she could be transported back in time to the days of knights and castles. Although the former English teacher's actual home is in Northeast Pennsylvania where she lives with her husband and two children, her online home can be found at CeceliaMecca.com. She would love to hear from you.

Stay in touch:
info@ceceliamecca.com

Made in the USA
Middletown, DE
21 November 2018